250 HOURS

COLLEEN NELSON

www.coteaubooks.com

250 HOURS

COLLEEN NELSON

Edited by Kathryn Cole
Cover designed by Scott Hunter
Text designed and typeset by Susan Buck
Printed and bound in Canada

Library and Archives Canada Cataloguing in Publication

Nelson, Colleen, author

     250 hours / Colleen Nelson.

Issued in print and electronic formats.

ISBN 978-1-55050-641-9 (pbk.).--ISBN 978-1-55050-648-8 (pdf).--
ISBN 978-1-55050-873-4 (epub).--ISBN 978-1-55050-880-2 (html)

     I. Title. II. Title: Two hundred fifty hours.

PS8627.E555T86 2015   jC813'.6   C2015-902919-8
                                                   C2015-902920-1

Library of Congress Control Number 2015938973

COTEAU BOOKS
2517 Victoria Avenue
Regina, Saskatchewan
Canada S4P 0T2
www.coteaubooks.com

10 9 8 7 6 5 4 3 2 1

Available in Canada from:
Publishers Group Canada
2440 Viking Way
Richmond, British Columbia
Canada V6V 1N2

Available in the US from:
Orca Book Publishers
www.orcabook.com
1-800-210-5277

Coteau Books gratefully acknowledges the financial support of its publishing program by: the Saskatchewan Arts Board, The Canada Council for the Arts, the Government of Canada through the Canada Book Fund, the City of Regina, and the Government of Saskatchewan through Creative Saskatchewan.

For my mom, Joan Chappell

CHAPTER 1

I JERKED AWAKE AT THE SUDDEN SILENCE. Staring at the baby monitor on my bedside table, I waited for Gam's next gurgly inhalation. It always came, but I worried about the day it didn't. How long can a heart pump in a 450-pound body?

Gam's resigned sigh echoed, electrified, through the monitor. Glancing at the clock, I realized she was awake and waiting for me to go downstairs and make her breakfast. Morbidly obese, hungry and trapped in a bed a few feet from the kitchen – the irony wasn't lost on me.

"Morning, Gam," I said as I stumbled past her room, my face swollen with sleep.

"Good morning, love," Gam called in her sweet, sing-song voice, just like she had every morning since I could remember. All the family I had left and I wouldn't have traded an ounce of her, not after everything she'd done for me.

My mom left when I was two months old. I look like her – blond hair, pale skin, blue eyes and slim. But even in photos of her as a child, my mother had a defiant tilt to her chin and a devilish gleam in her eye. My gleam, if I even had one, is more wistful than mischievous.

After so many years, I'd given up on a tearful, apologetic reunion. The realist in me understood why my mom left me here with Gam. She was seventeen. How could she have looked after a baby? Especially in Edelburg, where the probing eyes of neighbours are quick to judge and slow to forget.

After filling up the kettle for tea, I flicked on the radio to the sound of jovial patter about the price of grain and the weather. Gam liked to hear the local news first thing in the morning, even though not much happened in Edelburg, population 1,867, between the hours of 10 p.m. and 7 a.m.

Leaning against the counter, I waited for the water to boil. The view from the window above the sink was like a painting of a summer day. Framed by tall poplar and oak trees on either side, the grassy prairie stretched out behind the house marred only by our dilapidated garage that had paused mid-collapse.

I poured steaming water into two mugs and carried them into Gam's room, hip-checking the door to open it.

"Thanks, love," Gam said as I set her mug on the bedside table. "What would I do without you?" It was rhetorical. We both knew what would happen without me.

"Sleep okay?"

Gam nodded. The fat under her chin wobbled, but her head barely moved. She was encased in her own body, a prisoner of its suffocating weight.

When I was little, those fleshy arms encircled me in bed as she rocked me to sleep. I used to cushion myself in the pillowy softness of her stomach for movie marathons that stretched late into the night. She'd done her best to make my childhood a magical time. I didn't have a lot of friends, but she indulged my imagination, setting up fairy tea parties, complete with hand-sewn costumes and forts, in the living room. She'd never been like other grandmothers in town, spindly and bursting with energy. But Gam's quiet protectiveness had kept me safe and loved, despite everything. Sometimes, I wished there was still room in her bed for me to nestle against her. I could never love anyone as much as I loved Gam.

She was watching me, her eyes hidden beneath folds of skin. I smiled at her and put my feet up on her bed, leaning back in my chair. Her hand inched forward and rested on my bare ankle. The reassuring weight of her flesh seeped into me.

I slurped my tea, cringing at the scalding heat on my lips. "Aunt Mim will be here after lunch for your bath." The real appeal to her sister's visit wasn't the bath, but the gossip. A regular churchgoer, Mim would be bursting with news. And while they were hooting and chattering, I would be able to sneak upstairs and write in blissful, uninterrupted quiet.

I'd been working on my novel for two years and it was almost finished. A fantasy about a kidnapped princess who discovers she has magical powers, its convoluted story lines sometimes left me shaking my head, wondering how I would draw it to a close. Between school, my boyfriend, Rich, and looking after Gam most days, there wasn't time left for writing. But I'd graduated in June and summer holidays stretched in front of me, swollen with time. Rich didn't understand why I'd rather be inside, typing in Grandpa's office, than spending the day with him at the beach.

I'd explained to him how, after Grandpa died, losing myself in another world filled the space his death left in our lives. But I don't think Rich understood. Coming from a family of seven, he was an uncle three times over before he was twelve. His life was spent in a dizzying array of family celebrations: marriages, births, graduations, anniversaries, birthdays with a whirlwind of relations.

He'd never watched sickness strip someone he loved of their dignity until there was nothing left but a small, shriveled shell of a person. And the emptiness afterwards, when you cried so much you wondered how there could be any tears left. Rich had never been through that, either. I wondered if he ever would. You have to love someone a lot to know that kind of sadness.

Rich and I started dating the year Grandpa died. He said he'd never noticed me before, a typically blunt Rich thing to say. But all of a sudden, that year, I was on his radar. He'd seen me at the store, walking home from school, at church. I was probably mysterious to him, a girl removed from the social workings of Edelburg, and ripe for the picking. In a strange twist of fate, my body finally started to develop, curves replacing baby fat, at the same time as I lost my grandpa. I became someone worth looking at in a town of fresh-faced blonds.

He was a distraction too, at first, taking my mind off the sadness that pressed on my chest and made it hard to breathe. Gam was nervous about me dating. Rich was a few years older than me, and she'd eyed him warily when he first came over. But he'd worn her down and never once commented on her weight. I loved him for that, gratitude shining so bright it blinded me to other things. He was part of my life. An installation. Rich was comfortable and loyal and all the things a boyfriend should be.

"Sara Jean." Gam turned her eyes to the colostomy bag hidden under the sheets.

Sighing, I put down my mug. What *would* she do without me? My heart lurched at the thought of leaving Gam, but one day it would happen. Now that I'd graduated, she had to know it was only a matter of time. It was one of the few things we never spoke about. Maybe Gam thought if she didn't bring it up, it wouldn't occur to me.

Someone knocked on the screen door. Gam frowned at me and I shrugged. "Maybe it's Mim?" I hoped it wasn't some other relative or neighbour performing their monthly do-gooding. I'd have to invite them in for tea and a chat, and my whole morning of writing time would be wasted. Or was it Rich, surprising me with a trip to the beach? I groaned and hoped not. Telling him I couldn't go because I had to write would start an argument.

But, it wasn't a relative, or Rich. It was a tall, good-looking boy, on the cusp of being a man. He had dark brown eyes ringed by long eyelashes and looked at me as if I should know what he was doing on my front steps.

CHAPTER 2

Jess had planned on leaving this summer, hitchhiking to the city and saving enough to get somewhere good, like Vancouver. But last week, his plan had changed. The judge had glared at him from her desk as she reminded him he'd been caught for arson once before. If he hadn't been a minor, she would have recommended jail time. As it was, she added a lot more time to his community service hours. He shook his head at the total. Two hundred and fifty hours community service and twelve months probation. Jess wouldn't be going anywhere until his time was done.

His grandmother had stared at the floor when he told her about the punishment, disappointment etched on her face. He'd listened to her about staying away from other things, like booze and sniffing. But sometimes the urge to light a fire was too strong. It was like a snake slithering up his throat, desperate for escape. His whole body relaxed as the first weak flames licked at the wood. Watching the fire twist and crackle and gain strength was a release. He'd walk away able to handle life again, the snake sleeping contentedly in his belly.

The old shed had been irresistible, sitting in the middle of a field and set to be torn down the next day. He'd ridden his bike to it, a jar of gasoline sloshing as he swerved to avoid potholes in the gravel road. A crop plane had radioed down and before the fire had been able to take hold, a cop car, its siren blazing, had cornered him.

For 250 hours this summer, he'd be picking up trash on the highway, painting the high school, and clearing old shingles from the retirement home. Jonathan Fontaine was his social worker, eager to make a difference, one juvie at a time. He called Jess names such as Buddy and Dude, as if they were pals. He had even tried to do some weird fist-bump handshake thing the first time they met.

Jonathan had carried a blue file folder with Jess's name, spelled out with a Sharpie in capitals, the first time they'd met. He'd pulled out papers with signatures and a schedule for the community service hours and shown it to Jess. Two hundred and fifty hours, meant more than twenty hours a week for the entire summer. So much for hitching west. The first job was to clean out a garage for some old lady. Jess had shaken his head and groaned when he saw it was in Edelburg.

Walking through the town set him on edge. Everything was too perfect. Across the street, a sea of green front lawns and a few sprinklers spit blasts of water over flowerbeds – weeded and fertilized. A woman walking a dog on the sidewalk crossed to the other side as he approached.

He pulled the crumpled paper from his pocket and checked the address Jonathan had given him: 31 Winchester Lane. Set back from the road, the house had white siding and a porch that wrapped around the front and side. Some dried-out, gangly petunias grew in pots out front, but weeds had taken over the garden.

The screen door rattled in its frame when he knocked. A blond girl peered at him. She was tall and pale, like the under-side of a reed. There was a moment of silence as they stared at each other. It could have been the heat, but Jess preferred to think her cheeks flushed because of him.

Her almost invisible eyebrows wrinkled together. "Can I help you?"

"Uh, yeah," he said and cleared his throat. "I'm Jess Sinclair."

"Oh, right," she sighed. "Sorry. I forgot you were starting today. Can you go around the back? I'll be there in a minute."

"It's the kid doing community service," he heard her call to someone inside. *I'm not a kid*, he thought indignantly. Probably the same age as she was. "Remember, the firebug?" There was a pause. "Gam" – she sounded exasperated – "he's not going to set fire to a place he's working in… I know, I will be."

Jess gritted his teeth. He jumped off the porch and walked around to the back. It was going to be a long 250 hours.

CHAPTER 3

I HADN'T BEEN IN THE GARAGE FOR YEARS. Dust exploded around us as Jess heaved the door open. The earthy smell of damp cardboard and newsprint floated in the air. One window was broken, and the other two were so dusty they repelled the sun's attempt to shine in. There were boxes stacked on top of each other in towers as tall as me. I'd forgotten how much stuff there was.

"Anything worth keeping can go over there," I said, pointing to the windbreak of poplar trees separating our property from the neighbour's. "The rest can go to the dump."

He nodded and wiped his arm across his forehead. "Hot one today," he said and took off his shirt. I stared at him in horror and felt a crimson flush spread up my neck and over my cheeks. What was he doing? It was bad enough to have a delinquent working in the garage, but now he was parading around half-naked. All the neighbours would see him.

He tucked his shirt into the back pocket of his shorts, pushed some boxes out of the way and moved past me to see farther into the garage. Was that a smirk on his face?

"So, uh, I guess you can get started," I said without looking at him. "I'll be back later."

"Hey, what's your name?" he called after me.

"Sara Jean," I said, turning around. "Do you want anything? A glass of water?" *A shirt?*

He gave me a cocky smile. "Nah, I'm good."

I continued walking to the house.

Neighbours, full of concern, would be calling to inform me that a shirtless boy, who looked like he might be from the reserve, was working in the garage.

I dug around in a closet and found a stand-up fan and an extension cord and marched back to the garage. I plugged it in and the whir of the blades cut through the stillness of the air.

"What's that for?"

"To cool you off. So you can put your shirt back on." His tanned skin glowed like melted caramel. He looked at me like I was joking.

"I'm serious," I said. "You don't know my neighbours." I could feel the flush spreading up my cheeks.

He shook his head but yanked the shirt out of his pocket and pulled it on. "Better?" he asked.

"Thank you," I said, satisfied.

"I'm supposed to…" He pulled a folded paper out of his pocket. "Do you have a pen or something?"

I took the paper from him. His full name 'Jesse Augustine Sinclair' was printed in bold letters across the top. A chart below had space to record the date and hours worked. There was also a box for comments. *Needs to wear a shirt.*

"It has to be signed every day," he mumbled without meeting my eyes.

I pushed back a wave of sympathy and reminded myself why he was here. He'd committed a crime. But with the paper in my hand and the mountain of boxes behind him, I couldn't help feeling sorry for him. This wasn't how he wanted to spend his summer holidays.

It wasn't how I wanted to spend mine, either. "I have work to do inside," I told him. "Just knock if you want me, uh, need me. Or anything." Turning on my heel before I could make a bigger ass of myself, I left him with the whir of the fan and the smell of disintegrating cardboard.

So much for writing, I thought as the screen door slammed

behind me. It was mid-morning and I hadn't even turned on my computer yet. Gam needed breakfast, and the kitchen had to be tidied before Aunt Mim arrived.

"Love?" Gam called. "Did he start clearing out the garage?" Her eyes widened with curiousity. Her skin, once pale like mine, now stretched red and shiny across the fat. Years of neglect had left her light brown hair a stringy, greasy mess shot through with grey. Fingernails, ears, eyebrows had all stayed the same as the fat had taken over and all her appendages now looked comically small, dwarfed by her body.

I'd found her on the couch one day after school, damp with sweat, the colour drained from her cheeks. At first, I'd thought she was having a diabetic attack, that she'd forgotten to check her insulin. But no. It was the effort of lugging herself the few steps between the kitchen and the living room. Human bones, lungs, and heart aren't made to carry 450 pounds.

When Grandpa came home from golfing, he set up a bed in the TV room and called Aunt Mim. It took all three of us to propel Gam those few feet to her new room. As the days stretched into weeks and then months, the temporary bed became permanent. Gam filled the small room with her bulk and chirpy voice, glossing over the reality that she'd never walk again – not unless she lost some weight.

When Grandpa died, the minister performed a special service for Gam alone. Trapped by her own bulk, she couldn't go to her husband's funeral. She'd grieve alone, separate from the people who had known Grandpa their whole lives. I thought it might be the wake-up call she needed to make a change.

But it did the opposite. In her grief, she clung to what comfort she had, me and food, holding us both in a suffocating grip. Her room became a protective cocoon from the outside world.

"Sara Jean?" she said, pulling me out of my thoughts. She wanted details about the garage, the boy cleaning it and contents that no one had looked through in years. It would be easier if Jess did torch it. Save us all a big headache.

"I forgot how much stuff was in there," I said. "It's a big job."

Gam fiddled with the blankets, twisting them between her fingers. "You won't let him throw anything away, will you? We should go through the boxes to make sure there's nothing we want to keep."

"It's just Gramp's work stuff, files, things like that," I told her. "Nothing important."

"You never know," she warned. "Grandpa was such a packrat."

"What do you want me to do? Go through every box?" I said it sarcastically, but she turned to me with a grateful smile.

"That's probably a good idea. I'd hate to lose something that was important to Grandpa, wouldn't you?" Gam smiled sweetly, her cheeks dimpling as if she was a toddler, not a sixty-year-old woman.

Swallowing back my frustration, I set my mouth in a thin, annoyed line. "So now I'm doing community service too?" *On top of caring for you full-time.*

"Don't be silly. Just poke through the boxes and make sure he doesn't squirrel away any treasures."

A silent scream echoed between my ears. *Go supervise him yourself,* I wanted to shout at her, but of course I couldn't.

Gam turned up the volume on the TV and smoothed out the blankets she'd coiled around her fingers.

As I left the room, I put an imaginary red X through Writing Day 1.

CHAPTER 4

THE DUST MADE JESS'S EYES WATER. He'd stopped to wipe them when he heard glasses clink behind him. Sara Jean set a tray with a pitcher of iced tea down on a stack of boxes. "Help yourself," she said.

He poured a tall glass and downed it.

"It's hot out," she murmured as she sipped hers slowly.

"No bugs, though." The dry summer had kept the mosquitos at bay. Hundreds of dragonflies patrolled the sky, diving to catch what they could. Jess wondered how they never crashed. He poured himself some more iced tea and drank it slowly.

Jess wished she'd go back inside. He didn't want to spend his time making small talk. They sat in silence, watching condensation drip off their glasses. Jess traced a pattern in the water droplets and then wiped his chilled fingertips across his forehead.

"Do you go to Edelburg High?" she asked, squinting at him as the sun shone in her eyes. Strands of her hair glowed whitish-blond, like the filament in a light bulb.

"Nah, on the reserve." He waited for her reaction. Usually townies frowned at the mention of Deep River, a reserve only a few kilometres north of Edelburg. With run-down houses, dirt roads and old cars and used furniture littering yards, it was as different from the tidiness of Edelburg as it could get. Even though Jess lived in the trailer park between Edelburg and Deep River, he'd spent most of his life on the reserve at his kokum's home. It was Kokum, his grandmother, who had advised Jess's mom to send him to school on the reserve, where no one would judge a "half-breed" who lived in a trailer park. Jess's mom, Metis herself, had listened to Kokum. She knew what it was like to straddle two worlds. Better to pick one and embrace it than try to be part of both.

"Thought so. You didn't look familiar. Do you live on Deep River?" she asked, curiosity plain on her face.

He swirled the last drops of iced tea in the bottom of his glass and tipped it back, crunching on the melted shards of ice. "Kind of."

Sara Jean wrinkled her eyebrows at his cryptic answer and didn't ask any more questions. "My gam wants me to check the boxes before they go to the dump."

"She worried I'm gonna steal something?" Jess's tone turned combative, and Sara Jean took a step back.

She shook her head. "No. I – she – we want to know what's in the boxes, that's all." Her cheeks flared as Jess stared at her. Without looking at him, she picked up the tray and walked back to the house.

Nothing in this town ever changes, Jess thought, his anger rising. *As soon as they see an Indian, everyone locks their doors. May as well steal something since she thinks I'm going to anyway.* Jess was pulling back the cardboard flaps of a box when the bass and thump of a car's sound system made him pause. Peering through a grimy window, he watched as a Chevy Avalanche, white with high-end hubcaps that glittered in the sun, pulled up to the house.

Jess snorted when he saw who got out of the vehicle. Rich Wiens. Rich's face and neck were sunburned, probably from too much time golfing, or polishing his precious truck. People on the reserve joked that even if a townie's house was a wreck, they always had a new car washed and on display in their driveway. Edelburg had more car dealerships than stop signs.

Rich was the worst kind of townie. He looked at kids from Deep River like they were shit on the bottom of his shoe. Jess remembered walking around Rich's dad's dealership with Silas, a buddy who'd made some money working up north. Silas wanted to buy a car, but Rich had kicked them out, told them to get off his property or he'd call the cops.

Jess had tried to light a fire in a garbage can that day. It had smoked and fizzled, too damp to catch. Frustrated and angry, Jess had gone back to the dealership at night and keyed three cars. As Rich spun his keys on his finger and sauntered up to Sara Jean's house, an impulse made Jess emerge from the garage. Maybe he couldn't start fires, but he could set off some sparks.

Rich stopped and stared, shock evident on his face. In a moment, his expression turned to hostility as he curled his lips and let a bullet of spit fly from his mouth. "What the hell?"

The front door opened and Sara Jean flew down the stairs. She grabbed Rich's arms. "What are you doing?" she hissed.

"What's he doing here?" Rich seethed.

"Community service. Remember, I told you someone was clearing out the garage?"

Jess smirked as Rich looked like he wanted to punch something – or someone. "How long's he going to be here?"

Sara Jean shrugged. "Not long. A couple of days to clear it out and then haul stuff to the dump. Can you come inside? The neighbours are going to see you."

He pulled Sara Jean closer to him and spoke to her quietly. She nodded, her eyes wide and trusting. Jess turned away and walked back to the garage when Rich leaned in to kiss her.

Fucking prick. It was guys like Rich that made Jess want to burn the whole town to the ground. Teach them all a lesson. The urge to hear the match strike and smell the sulphur as it ignited made his fingers itch.

But he'd promised Kokum no more. There'd be no more fires. If he got caught, it would mean jail time, and he didn't want to become another statistic. Instead, he kicked a box again and again, his frustration battering the cardboard. Glass shattered and spilled out the hole his foot had made.

CHAPTER 5

RICH'S SURPRISE VISIT HAD LEFT A SICK FEELING in my stomach. He'd told me to fire Jess. Actually, he'd demanded it. I hadn't argued, not outside with Jess a few metres away, but he wasn't working in Rich's garage, he was working in mine. Shouldn't it be my decision?

I hated arguing with Rich, and I usually let him have his way to avoid it. Or I kept things like Jess working in the garage and my university application a secret.

I'd have to tell him soon though, since my letter of acceptance to the University of Manitoba had arrived, and, based on my marks, I was eligible for a scholarship. I had to give the university an answer by the end of July.

My going to university didn't fit into Rich's plan for us. He wanted to get married, buy a house and take over his dad's car dealership. In his future vision of us, we had kids, and I stayed at home to raise them, just like his mom had. For a lot of girls in Edelburg, watching their boyfriends' eyes light up with excitement at the thought of backyard barbeques and white picket fences was a dream come true. Not me. Every time Rich started talking about our life together, now that I was finished high school, I felt a knot in my stomach. How could I tell the person I love that his perfect future sounded like a punishment?

I hadn't told Gam about university, either. In a lot of ways, it would be easier not to go. But that meant giving up on my dreams of being a writer and resigning myself to a life in

Edelburg as Mrs. Rich Wiens.

With a start, I glanced at the clock and realized Gam needed to eat soon. Her insulin levels had to be tested on a regular schedule, and she needed to eat every few hours. Making food for someone obese felt pointless. Why bother when she already weighed so much? But if I didn't, Gam's body would go into shock and she'd have a seizure. It had happened a few months ago. I'd been writing on a Saturday and lost track of time. I'd found her trembling, covered in sweat, with her eyes rolled back in her head.

I hadn't slept for weeks after, nervous that it would happen again.

"Gam, lunch." I nudged the door open and put the tray down on the table. Gam tilted her head to peer at the plate. "Mmm. Ham. Thank you, love."

"Do you want a drink?"

Gam turned back to the TV. "Some iced tea would be lovely. Can you pass me my tester kit? I need to check my levels."

I handed it to her. Gam's hands shook with the effort of reaching and sitting up to grab it. The physiotherapist had suggested making her work for things, not just handing them over, but I'd seen the look of disgust cross the woman's face when she walked into Gam's room. I know what strangers think when they look at Gam: a blob lying in bed, too stubborn or lazy to get up. But it wasn't Gam's fault that her body didn't work how it was supposed to. If she'd been bedridden because of multiple sclerosis or something, people would look at her with pity, not revulsion.

"I'm going to write after lunch, but I'll listen for Aunt Mim, okay?"

Gam chewed the sandwich daintily. "Okay, dear. What's his name?"

"Who?"

"The boy cleaning the garage."

"Jess something. I can't remember his last name."

"Is he from the reserve?"

I hesitated. Gam blinked, waiting for an answer.

"He lives in the trailer park, but he goes to school on Deep River."

She shook her head and muttered, "I figured. It's always those kids causing trouble."

There was a knock at the back door. "Hello?" Jess called. "Hello?"

Through the screen, his body looked like a hulking shadow. As I got closer, I could see his face was slick with perspiration and there were dark patches of sweat on his shirt. I felt a flash of guilt that he had to work outside in the heat all day.

"Can I have a glass of water?" he asked through the screen.

"Yeah, hang on." I let the tap water run so cold that it numbed my fingers. "Here you go." I opened the door and handed the glass to him. The odour of tangy sweat, not yet pungent, swirled around him. He drank the water in one long gulp, his throat convulsing with each swallow.

He let out a sigh of relief when he'd finished and handed the glass back to me. "Thanks."

I turned to go back inside.

"Guess your boyfriend wasn't too happy to see me." There was a cocky glint in his eye.

I paused. "Not really."

"So why don't you fire me?"

Sighing, I let the screen door rest against my foot and straddled the threshold. "I need the garage cleaned out. And it's not up to Rich." I sounded tougher than I felt. I also knew that if Rich pushed me on it again, I'd give in.

I thought Jess would walk away, but he didn't. Hooking his hands around the porch railing, he leaned back, relaxed and chatty. "You fish?"

I gave him a confused look, frustration growing at the thought of the computer humming with electricity upstairs and the empty chair in front of it.

He grinned and a dimple appeared in his cheek. "There's some old fishing rods in the garage."

"They're my grandpa's. I've never been."

"You've *never* been fishing? You live ten minutes from Deep River. You shitting me?"

I shook my head.

"Your grandpa never took you? Or your dad?"

Bristling at the mention of my dad, a man I'd never met, who didn't know I existed, I gripped the door frame. "I've got things to do. Do you want more water, or…" I let my question trail off, hoping he'd take the hint.

He did. The grin disappeared and he shook his head.

From the window, I watched him go into the garage. *I should have been friendlier,* I berated myself. What if Gam was right and there was something of value? He had every reason to take it after I'd dismissed him like a servant.

Before I could think too much more about it, I found myself walking across the yard, wilting in the humidity. "Jess?" I called quietly. He jumped off the box he'd been sitting on, an old comic in his hands.

Pursing my mouth, I raised an eyebrow. "I didn't mean to be rude. Your question about my dad caught me off guard, that's all." A hot flush spread up my face. "My mom left when I was a baby. I never met my dad."

Jess bent toward me, like he was waiting for me to say something else. "That's it?" he asked with a raised eyebrow. "You looked so freaked out, I thought you were going to tell me he was an alien or something."

I gave him a weak smile. At least there'd been no sympathetic shake of the head. My admission hadn't fazed him.

"So you live with your grandparents?"

"My grandma. Grandpa died a couple of years ago. This is all his stuff.

Jess slapped the comic book against a box, missing a fly. "I kind of live with my grandma too. Used to sleep over all the time when I was kid when my mom had to work late. My dad ditched out on me too. I think he's in Winnipeg, maybe Regina." Jess ran a hand through his hair, making it stand on end in short, shiny spikes. I wondered if he was telling me all this to put me at ease or to avoid working.

"Why did he leave?" I asked.

Jess shrugged. "Don't know. The usual."

I didn't know what "the usual" was. In Edelburg, parents didn't abandon their children. Well, most parents, anyway.

"You ever hear from her, your mom?"

Biting the insides of my cheeks, I shook my head. *Not a word or a phone call in my whole life.* I sighed. "Sometimes I wonder if she's...not around anymore." I couldn't bring myself to say 'dead'. "It would explain why she never came back. But then, I'd never know why she left, either." I didn't know why I was telling him all this. I hadn't even told Rich my fears about my mom, not that he'd ever asked.

"At least it would explain why she never came back."

"But then I'd never know why she left, either." I didn't know why I was telling him all this. I hadn't even told Rich my fears about my mom.

Jess's attention turned to the street, where a dusty blue Cadillac, circa 1985, pulled up to the curb. "Is that another boyfriend?" he asked.

I peeked around the corner of the garage, my stomach dropping. "Worse. Aunt Mim."

"WHO'S THAT BOY?" Aunt Mim hollered to me as I walked across the yard to greet her.

"An indentured servant. Do you need help with anything?"

"There's a casserole in the backseat. What's he doing here? You didn't let him in the house, did you?" Mim had lived in the city for years but moved back to Edelburg to teach at the high school and to keep an eye on Gam. It was hard to believe Mim and Gam were sisters. Mim was rail thin and boney, with brown hair clipped short. Her wardrobe consisted entirely of tracksuits in bright colours. Today's was bright pink with a turquoise stripe.

"He's cleaning out the garage," I told her, my voice muffled by twenty-five-year-old velvet upholstery as I grabbed the casserole. "Remember? For his community service."

"*Humph.* Just so long as he stays out where we can see him," she said with her hands on her hips. "We need to talk about something." She closed the car door for me. "Lucy Friesen told me you got a letter from the university."

I almost dropped the casserole. "What? How does she know that?"

"Shush! Her husband, Fred, sorts the mail when old Mr. Friesen is on holidays. Anyway, that's not the point. I want you to know that I think" – she paused dramatically – "it's a great idea! The best thing I ever did was move to the city. And don't you worry about your Gam. We'll sort something out – maybe get someone from the church to pop in and give her meals when I can't make it." Mim's eyes shone with excitement for me, but I felt like I'd been punched in the stomach. This wasn't the way I wanted people to find out: from the replacement mail sorter.

"I haven't decided anything yet. And don't you tell Gam!" I admonished Mim. "I haven't even told Rich." Marching up the front steps, I threw a warning look at her and went inside.

Bath time was never fun for anyone except Gam. It took two of us to roll her over and wet and lather her up, taking care to wash under each fold and then carefully dry the skin and put ointment on the bedsores. One of us held Gam on her side while the other one changed the sheets. Afterwards, Gam glowed pink, and the room smelled like Vaseline and chamomile soap until the next day, when the sour smell of obesity returned.

Finally, I retreated to the computer room, which used to be my grandpa's study. He'd been a teacher and loved history,

especially of southern Manitoba and its Mennonite immi-
grants, and his books filled the shelves. There was still a row of
his journals that he'd kept for his whole life, leather-bound and
filled with spidery handwriting.

Photos of our family cluttered the walls, along with some
yellowed maps and a black-and-white picture of his parents.
The huge wooden desk under the window had turned legs and
heavy drawers I had to heave it open with both hands. I could
see the horizon from up here, where land meets sky, a magical,
untouchable place.

Settling into the old office chair, I stretched out my fingers
and listened as my computer hummed to life. A picture of Rich
and I flashed on the screen. He'd surprised me with the computer last Christmas, waiting until everyone else had finished
opening their presents. I'd thought he'd given it to me as a way
of saying he supported my writing, but as his family shook
their heads at his generosity, I wondered if his grand gesture
was more for him than for me.

I stared at the screen. Sixty-seven thousand words were
behind me. I estimated I needed another five or six thousand
to tie up the plot and give my characters satisfying endings. All
I needed to do was concentrate and float away to the world I'd
created with letter keys and a space bar. But I couldn't. As my
fingers ran over the keys, I felt the energy drain out of me.
Some days, it was slow torment forcing myself to write, and
other days, I couldn't type fast enough to catch all the thoughts
spilling from my head. My shoulders slumped when I realized
today was not one of those days.

From my window, I watched Jess add another box to the
pile in the yard. I'd never met another person who'd been aban-
doned by their parent. I knew there had to be others, but not in
Edelburg. Spinning around in my chair, I planted my feet on
the floor and decided to do what I'd promised Rich I wouldn't.

Carrying an armload of rusty farm equipment, Jess looked
up when the screen door snapped shut behind me.

He wiped the sweat off his forehead. "Mind if I head out? I wanna try out that rod of your grandpa's." I raised my eyebrows in surprise, hoping to hide my disappointment. He faced me, squinting into the sun. "Wanna come?"

"Fishing?" I asked, my eyes wide at his boldness. He knew I had a boyfriend. "I can't. Gam might need me," I stammered. Cursing my fair skin, I felt a blush spread up my neck and over my face.

"I was joking," he said and threw me a look that made me blush three shades deeper. A thin film of sweat coated his face, gluing bits of dust and dirt to his skin. "Uh, did you sign that paper?" he asked. Jess twirled the rod in his hands, his eyes carefully avoiding mine. "My social worker might ask for it."

"It's inside. It says to submit it to Jonathan Fontaine when the work is complete." *And, at four hours a day, that was going to take a while.*

He picked up the fishing rod and tucked it under his arm. "See you tomorrow," he said and sauntered toward the sidewalk.

I pulled my eyes away from his departing back and looked around. He'd started sorting, pushing boxes to one side of the garage and everything else to the other. The boxes were stacked four or five high. The one with comic books sat open. I shook my head, wondering if he'd done anything but read them. Maybe I did need to stay out here to supervise, or the work would never get done.

I pulled a box toward me and opened it. Old curriculum, school policy booklets, attendance ledgers from the days before computers – why had Grandpa kept all this stuff? At the bottom of the box was another box, as if whatever was inside needed extra protection. I lifted the lid. There was a package of black-and-white photos. The elastic holding them was dry and cracked. And there was a hardcover book with a gold cross embossed on the bottom right-hand corner.

I opened the book. Grandpa's name was written on the inside cover; it was his attendance log from 1967. Listed on each page were students' names, but the names were unfamiliar: Bear, Deerchild, Fontaine, Dumas, Mason, Thompson. These weren't Edelburg names, they were names found on the reserve.

The elastic snapped in half when I picked up the photos. The first picture showed solemn-faced, dark-haired boys and girls standing at attention on the front steps of a building. The date,1967, had been stamped at the bottom. I flipped through the package: girls working at sewing machines, heads down, like at a factory; groups of kids in winter clothing, flannel jackets and boots, huddled together beside a snow pile; a two-storey brick building. I squinted at the carved name above the door. Edelburg Residential School. The residential school? Foggy references to a school that had been closed down years ago, before I was born, filtered into my head.

"What are you doing?"

"You scared me!" I gasped.

Aunt Mim surveyed the boxes and the pile of artifacts I'd dug up. "What's all this mess? I thought you were clearing it out and sending it to the dump."

"Me too. Gam wanted to make sure there wasn't anything important."

Mim dropped down beside me and picked up the attendance ledger. The pile of photos on top slid off, scattering on the ground. I watched her brow furrow. She cast a swift glance at me and tossed the book aside. "It's a bunch of junk. Just cart it off to the dump, if you ask me. Alice will never know what was here, anyway." Mim's words sounded sure, but the way she chewed her lip and looked at the photos made me wonder if it really was junk.

"I don't mind," I shrugged. "It's kind of cool going through Grandpa's things."

"Seems a bit nosey, if you ask me."

I wondered if Mim knew the definition of *ironic*.

CHAPTER 6

THE DEEP RIVER SNAKES ITS WAY through the valley, leaving rocky outcrops perfect for fishing. Jess had been baking in the sun for over an hour, his line dangling in the water. A cloud of gnats moved in front of him, and he waved them away. Peeling off his clothes, he decided to jump in. If there weren't any fish, he didn't have to worry about scaring them away. Partway up the bank, he found a rock that stuck up like a hitchhiker's thumb and dove off it into the river below. The cool water rushed past him, swirling over his body. With a powerful kick, he burst through the surface and lay floating on his back. There was no better feeling than swimming in deep, fresh water and staring up at a cloudless sky.

He knew his dad used to come here to fish. Kokum had shown him the mark he'd made in a birch tree. GL. Jess had dug the initials out after his dad disappeared the last time. He didn't deserve to lay claim to this spot any more. He'd traded in swimming and fishing in the river for wandering the streets in Winnipeg.

Thinking about his dad was going to ruin the afternoon. Jess had seen others follow the same path, but that didn't make it any easier. He remembered his dad stumbling through the door in the middle of the night. He wasn't a loud, obnoxious drunk but a sullen, morose one. He'd collapse on the couch and stare at nothing, his eyes dark and haunted. A teacher had read a story about a monster that turned men to stone, and that's what his dad had looked like when he was drunk, hollow and empty.

He pushed the memories away. At least his dad hadn't left boxes of crap to sort through like Sara Jean's grandpa. He didn't understand why people held on to things. Maybe it was because they'd never had to let go of something important and thought things that could be boxed up mattered. They just ended up in a garage, being hauled off to the dump by a kid doing community service – probably not what the old guy'd had in mind when he left them.

Be a lot easier to just burn them. It would go up so quickly, with all the boxes and old papers. But torching the garage wouldn't be a thrill. He knew who it belonged to. He set fire to anonymous buildings, places to store his hurt and anger that he could watch burn without remorse.

Planting his feet carefully on the slippery rocks, he climbed to the shore and put on his clothes. It was a kilometre walk to his grandmother's house. He'd been hoping to drop a fresh fish on her doorstep and watch as she filleted it. A breeze stirred the tall grasses, and they rustled behind him like a chorus taunting him to stay. He baited his hook, cast one more time and let drops of river water trickle down his back.

The snap of a branch behind him made his heart jump. Jess turned around to find Tom Deerchild, Dustin Henry and his cousin Rufus Sinclair standing behind him, pointing sticks at him like spears.

"Fuck off, you losers."

The boys erupted into laughter. "Daydreaming, eh? We been here since you got out of the water. Rufus farted and you didn't hear us."

Jess stared out at the water, annoyed. He wished he'd left after his swim.

"Where were you all day? Your gran didn't know, eh." Tom had two older brothers who had left the reserve, and in their absence he'd assumed the role of ringleader for the Deep River

25

boys. The role didn't fit. He was wiry and scrappy but not much of a leader. The other two only followed him because they were lazy and couldn't be bothered finding someone else to attach themselves to.

Jess snorted and watched Tom from the corner of his eye. "Stuff to do in town. All your talking's scaring the fish."

"What's the excuse before we got here, eh?" Tom sneered. "You didn't catch nothing!"

As if on cue, Jess's line tensed and the rod curved to the water. He stood up and reeled some line in, then let the rod touch the surface, then pulled in some more. The gentle rocking motion teased the fish up until it popped from the water, squirming and jumping on the end of his line.

With one hand, Jess grabbed a knife out of his pocket, cut the line and let the fish fall to the ground. Air burned through its gills until finally the death dance ended and the fish lay still. It was a good size, and his grandmother would cluck at him when he walked in with it. She'd coat the fillet with cracker crumbs and fry it in a pan with butter. He could hear the sizzle as he watched the jealous glances of his friends.

"Suzie Miller's having a bonfire tonight. You goin'?" Rufus was two years younger than Jess. He was chubby and breathed through his mouth. Jess wondered if pickings were that slim at Deep River that Tom counted Rufus as one of his boys. No wonder Tom harassed Jess to hang out.

"Maybe." Jess picked up his catch and didn't look back as he walked through the grass and back to the main road. Hanging out with those jokers made him hate life on the reserve. Made him hate his dad. This was what he'd left Jess with.

Not that living in town was any better. Townies looked at him like he was an illiterate bum. Sometimes he snarled at them, but most of the time he met their eyes and gave them the once over. Most of them had never left Edelburg, would get married at nineteen, pop out a few kids and live within a two-minute drive of their parents. Not so different from the reserve, except they drove fancier cars and had nicer houses.

The cattails bent as he pushed his way through them. A few of their heads snapped back and pelted him with their bullet-shaped bodies. One popped and a cloud of fluff exploded around him. The late day sunlight cast its yellow haze over the dry prairie grass. Jess felt its heavy heat scorching his forehead as he walked home. His dad had left years ago for something else. Jess wondered if he'd ever found it.

His grandmother's house sat in the middle of the reserve. The uniform grey siding and roof didn't give a hint of the chaos that greeted Jess when he opened the door. Moose, deer and caribou antlers were nailed to the upper walls of the home beside a dreamcatcher and a plastic statue of Mary, in her blue robe, one hand outstretched and helpful. Crocheted blankets in a riot of colour lay over every piece of furniture, most to hide stains and tears in the fabric. Kokum's sewing, tiny pots of beads and lengths of pre-cut thread, spread across the table. Most of the moccasins she made ended up at the gas station, sold to people passing through. They'd been the only shoes Jess had worn when he was little. Even now, a pair sat under his bed. He'd slip them on sometimes, or hold them up to his nose, breathing in the pungent odour of the animal hide.

A black wood stove, the only source of heat in the winter, sat in the middle of the room and separated the kitchen and living room. Three couches, fit arm to arm, stretched across one wall, and a row of wooden chairs lined the other.

Her home was the unofficial meeting place for members of the band, and her fridge was always stocked with visitors' gifts thanking her for her hospitality. The smell of oil-fried bannock had settled into the walls and floors of the home where she had raised six children. In the summer, electric fans whirled and wind chimes in front of the screens tinkled like breaking glass.

"Kokum? Are you here?" Jess shouted. No one locked their doors on the reserve.

"Out here!"

He turned to see his grandmother hauling an axe from the shed. She dropped it beside a tree trunk. Jess groaned.

"Need to split the logs. We're having a bonfire."

"When?"

"Soon." She took the fish from Jess and into her house. "Nice."

"How'd she even know I was coming over?" he muttered under his breath as he grabbed some birch logs from the pile under a tarp. He knew his well-muscled arms were due to the chores – hauling water, chopping logs, shovelling snow – that she had made him do since he was a kid. But, with the late day sun beating down on him, he wished he'd stayed by the water a little longer, even if it meant hanging out with the Deep River boys.

"That's enough," his grandmother called from out the window when he'd chopped up half the log pile. "Dinner's ready."

She'd made one of his favourite meals: breakfast for dinner. A plate of pancakes slathered with syrup and butter lay in the middle of the table, and he had smelled the salty fried bacon from outside.

"Thanks."

The vinyl kitchen chairs had been around as long as Jess could remember, and each seat was perfectly worn where a person's butt needed to be. The legs had scraped grooves in the linoleum floor from being pushed in and out so often.

They ate in silence. Jess's fork scratched against his plate as he drew circles in the syrup with his pancake. It wasn't uncommon for the two of them to go through a whole meal without saying anything. When he ate with his mom, she wanted to know all about his day and what he had planned for tomorrow. She'd tell him stories about the people who came into the restaurant and vent about her boss or the cook and his wandering hands.

"I was thinking, maybe I'd go to Winnipeg or Vancouver or something, you know, to live for a while. After the community service is done."

Kokum didn't look at him. She speared a piece of soggy pancake and let the syrup drip off it. "What for?"

Jess shrugged. "See what it's like. Get a job."

"Up to you."

"You think it's a good idea?"

She finished chewing her bite. "Seen a lot of people go to the city, eh? Not many come back."

Jess grinned. "Worried you're gonna miss me?" he teased and reached for another pancake.

"Save money on food at least," she deadpanned. But she gave Jess a solemn look. "Your home is here."

Still chewing the last piece of bacon, his grandmother went into the fridge and pulled out a bottle of pop and some cakes in cellophane wrappers. Jess pressed the package until the air exploded and the cake burst out. His grandmother smiled and her body quivered with a silent laugh as he let out a loud belch.

"You only catch the one?" She tilted her head to the fish lying in the sink.

"Yeah. Too hot."

She snorted. "Easy to make excuses. Didja try minnows?"

"Nah. Didn't have any."

"I got some in the freezer." She nodded with her chin. "Old Boney Stevens brought them over."

"I'll bring them next time. Not sure how much fishing I'll get to do anyhow, with the community service."

His grandmother didn't acknowledge him, but that didn't mean she hadn't heard.

Actually, Jess thought his kokum listened better than anybody.

CHAPTER 7

THE MORNING SUN CAST SHAFTS OF LIGHT on the hardwood floor of my room, and I arched my back like a cat in one final stretch. The night air had barely cooled the house; my room still felt stuffy. I didn't bother to put on my bathrobe when I heard Gam wake up. Modesty between Gam and me had been lost the first time I emptied her bedpan.

"Morning, love. Is the tea on yet?" Gam used one of her honey-sweet voices, which meant she wanted something now but would never demand it.

"Just starting it."

"You slept in."

"I did? What time is it?"

"Half past eight. That boy is going to be here soon."

I squeezed my eyes shut and groaned. Water sloshed into the kettle as I filled it up, put it on to boil, turned on the radio and started a mental checklist of all I wanted to do today. If I'd gotten up on time, I could have finished the housework early and spent the rest of the morning writing before helping Gam in the afternoon. It was physiotherapy today and the library books were due. Rich's parents had invited me to dinner, so I'd have to get something for Gam before I left. Would Writing Day 2 have another X through it?

I plopped a tea bag in the pot and slathered two pieces of toast with butter and marmalade. I poured the steaming hot water into the teapot and fit the knitted tea cozy over it and carried the breakfast tray into Gam's room just as the doorbell rang. I froze. "I – I can't get the door."

"Why not?"

"Gam!" I laughed. "Look at me! I'm in my underwear!"

"Just a minute," I yelled at the door, not sure if Jess could hear me. Who ever heard of a delinquent showing up early to do community service?

The teacup clattered against the saucer as I put the tray down and scurried upstairs. My hair was tangled in a puff of blond at the back of my head, and I had morning breath. I threw on a pair of sweats and a hoodie, pulling my hair into a ponytail as I walked back down the stairs.

When I opened the door, nobody was there. Sliding on a pair of flip-flops, I stepped outside. "Jess?" I called.

He poked his head out of the garage. "I rang the doorbell, but no one answered, so I thought I'd get to work while it's a bit cooler. Gonna be hot today, eh?"

"Uh, yeah."

He raised an eyebrow at me. "Why are you wearing sweats? It's like thirty degrees out already." The white muscle shirt he wore looked cool and bright against his skin.

"I know. I should go change." *And shower, and brush my teeth.* I cringed at the thought of what I must look like, turned on my heel and marched back to the house.

Gam was on the phone. I knew it was Aunt Mim because of the elongated "oh's" and "really's".

"Love, can you come in here a minute?" The cordless handset lay nestled between her chin and shoulder. "Mim says you found some boxes of school papers."

I nodded.

"You don't need to go through those, love." Gam wrinkled her nose in disgust. "That boy can take them to the dump."

"What if there's something worth keeping?"

Gam pursed her lips. "There won't be."

"I found some things from the residential school. I didn't

know Grandpa taught there."

Gam stared at me for a minute and then put the phone back to her ear. "I'll call you later, Mim." She wound the sheet around her fingers. "What did you find?"

"Photos, his attendance book."

Gam let out a sigh. "I don't know why he hung on to all those things. Working at that school did nothing but make him upset. He only lasted the one year, but it left a mark on him."

"What do you mean?"

Gam's hair curled around her face in sweaty ringlets. "Things went on at that school that Grandpa couldn't understand. They didn't treat the children properly, poor things. They'd been sent there, some of them hundreds of miles away from their families. I don't know how any mother could do that to her children. Desert them like that."

My eyes fell to the floor. Mothers deserting their children was a sore subject for me.

Gam shut her eyes and her chin quivered. "Oh, love. I didn't mean anything about you. It was different with your mother."

I raised an eyebrow and snorted. "Not really."

Gam sputtered, trying to think of something to say.

Before I left her room, I turned back. "Could you have done what she did? Left your child?"

Gam met my eyes and I held her gaze. "No," she whispered.

"I didn't think so," I said and went upstairs to change.

CHAPTER 8

SARA JEAN CAME BACK OUTSIDE IN A TANK TOP and cut-off shorts. The pale pink top disappeared against her skin. She sat on the ground, twisting her legs like a pretzel and pulled a box toward her without saying a word.

They worked silently for a while until she pulled out a sheaf of papers. "Do you know anything about the Edelburg Residential School?" she asked, looking up at him with watery blue eyes.

"Yeah."

"Like what? Who was it for? Who worked there?"

Jess hesitated, not sure if he wanted to get into this with her. But she kept staring at him, waiting, so Jess walked over and sat on the ground beside her. "They were for Indian kids, to teach them how to be white."

She grabbed a pile of photos from the box beside her. "I found these yesterday." She leaned over to show him. Jess saw that the skin of her cheeks was lightly freckled. He'd never been close enough to notice that before. "That" – she pointed at a man, young, with slicked-back dark hair, smiling at the camera – "is my grandpa."

Jess took the photo from her. Rows of Indian kids stood on the steps of a school. It was grainy, but he looked closely. Could one of the boys wearing stiff denim pants have been his dad?

Jess had hung out at the school. Now it was a place for kids to go if they wanted to get high or messed up. Overrun by rodents, weeds and graffiti, it loomed over a bend in the Deep River, a silent reminder of suffering for families on the reserve. The band had been asking to have it torn down for years, but the government hadn't done anything about it.

"He taught at the school?" Jess asked.

"Yeah, I never knew till I found this stuff yesterday. Gam said he only lasted a year. He didn't like how parents sent their kids away to the school instead of keeping them at home."

Jess snorted in disbelief.

"That's what Gam told me," she said, straightening her back.

He shook his head. "Those kids were *forced* to go by the church or the government. Sometimes, the kids just got taken if the parents wouldn't send them." Jess scowled. Townies lived with their heads up their asses. "Kokum had to send all her kids to that school. My dad's brother Phil died there."

"Oh." She put the photos back in the box.

Jess kept talking. "They used to try to beat the 'savage' out of the kids. Made them stand with piss-stained sheets over their head if they wet the bed."

"My grandpa would never have done that." She shook her head stubbornly, cutting him off.

Jess set his mouth in a smirk.

"He wouldn't have done things like that," she repeated, the colour rising in her cheeks. "It's a dumb thing to argue about. Neither of us was there, so we'll never know."

Jess turned back to the garage and removed his shirt just to piss her off.

CHAPTER 9

MY KNEES CRACKED WHEN I STOOD UP. We'd been working silently all morning. Instead of mindlessly thumbing through papers, I'd started to hunt for documents that would prove Grandpa wasn't a monster, that he hadn't mistreated children at the residential school. Or better yet, that Jess was wrong, and the school wasn't as bad as he thought. So far, I hadn't found anything. Maybe Jess was being dramatic about kids being stolen from their families. People in town wouldn't have allowed it to go on if they had known, would they?

I checked to see if the angry furrow in Jess's brow was gone. As he walked past me, I heard a loud gurgling, like the engine of a motorboat sputtering.

"Was that your stomach?"

"Uh, yeah." He didn't look at me, but his face relaxed. "I didn't eat breakfast."

"I'll go make lunch," I said, relieved to have an end to the tension.

Inside, the quick chatter of a talk show murmured through the house. Gam stayed asleep when I put the tray of food on her bedside table, her breathing choked and jumpy as usual. Her levels needed to be checked. I glanced at the clock. That could wait another half hour until Jess and I had eaten and I brought the empty plates inside.

Stepping outside was a relief. The air conditioner made the house unnaturally frigid, and I let the heat suffocate the chill out of me.

I'd ignored Jess's shirtlessness while we'd been working, but couldn't now. His skin was shiny with sweat, and rivulets ran down his neck and into the crease between his shoulder blades.

"Thanks," he said and grabbed a sandwich, taking it with him as he moved into the shade of the garage. I slid onto the ground and leaned against a stack of boxes, conscious of keeping some distance between us. It was one thing to be working outside near him, but I should have eaten inside, alone. Not outside with him.

Jess sat with his arms hanging over his bent knees. "What do you do for fun around here?" he asked, taking a bite of sandwich.

"Fun? In Edelburg?"

He smirked at my sarcasm. I remembered the day the high school held its first dance. I'd been in grade two! The town's squeaky-clean image was more important than letting teenagers gyrate to loud music. With only a strip mall, gas station, Chinese restaurant and two antique stores in the downtown, there wasn't much to do in Edelburg except hang out at the ice-cream stand in the summer or watch movies in the winter. "I like to write," I told him.

"Yeah? What kind of writing?"

"Um." I hesitated. Trying to explain what I wrote about would feel pretentious, as if I was claiming to be a famous novelist.

He was waiting for me to speak.

"I've written some short stories, but right now I'm working on a novel."

Jess wasn't fazed. He nodded and reached for a bottle of water. "What are the short stories about?" he asked.

"About Edelburg. There's a lot that goes on around here that no one talks about. One is about my mom." I'd never told anyone about that story. Not even Gam. "I thought it might help to write about it."

He took a long drink but kept his eye trained on me. "I

guess we all have our own way of dealing with shit, huh?"

Like setting fires? I wondered.

Jess tipped his head back and chugged the rest of the water. He was good looking, that was for sure. But there was something unsettling in his eyes; they flashed on a dime between gentleness and anger, as if the two burned beneath the surface in equal parts.

"Deep River sucks too. Nothing to do, no jobs."

"Would you ever leave?"

He shrugged, stuffing the last bite of sandwich into his mouth. "Don't know. Thought about going out west to Vancouver or something. But then this happened." He waved his hand around, almost as if the garage was to blame. "You?"

I thought about the letter from the U of M sitting in my desk drawer. I'd reread it so many times the paper had softened along the edges. "I haven't decided yet. My grandma needs someone to look after her."

"What's wrong with her?"

"She's got diabetes." *And weighs 450 pounds.*

"Lots of people at Deep River have diabetes. She real sick or something?"

"Sort of."

The slam of a car door startled me. I peeked around the corner of the garage and saw Rich's truck. "Shit!" I scrambled up and raced to the garage.

Jess smirked as if he was enjoying my panic. I'd clamped a hand over my mouth and willed him to be quiet with my eyes. I should have known better! Of course Rich would check up on me. He'd said he was golfing all day with his dad. How could I have been so naïve?

My stomach twisted into knots. If Rich found me crouched in the corner of the garage, he'd be furious. The thought was humiliating. I hadn't done anything wrong, but that wasn't what he'd think.

I needed to dash for the back door. Had I unlocked it this

morning? What if he kept knocking, and Gam called out to him to come inside?

Oh my God, Gam! I hadn't gone back to check her levels. Scenarios ran through my head. She'd check before she ate lunch, she wasn't a child! But what if she couldn't reach the kit? What if she got so hungry she couldn't wait and ate before she tested? Blood hammered in my head. I needed to get out of here and check on her, even if it meant dealing with Rich.

Jess stood up and whistled. "Townie! Looking for your girlfriend?"

My eyes widened to twice their size. What was he doing?

"Yeah, I am." Rich's voice sounded like a fist, balled for a fight.

"Saw her leave a while ago. With some lady in a blue car."

I squeezed my eyes shut, praying that Rich would buy the lie.

Jess didn't move. He stood with his feet spread like an animal ready to fight for its territory.

Jess yelled a sarcastic "You're welcome". I heard Rich's truck door slam and his engine roar to life.

I counted to thirty and peeked out. Rich's truck was gone.

Jess stood with his hands on his hips, shaking his head at me.

"Don't say it," I said, holding up my hand. I had to get to Gam. I ran past him and took the stairs three at a time, bursting into the house and slamming my hands on the door frame to her bedroom to steady myself.

Gam turned to me with an angelic smile. "Oh love, did you see Rich? I heard him knocking."

I almost laughed with relief. "Yeah, I saw him." *When did lying become this easy?* "Did you check your levels?" I asked, noticing the crumbs left on the sandwich plate.

"A while ago. When you didn't come in, I thought I might have to call Mim to help me, but I managed."

"Sorry. I – the garage is a bigger job than I thought."

She leaned her head back into the pillow. "I hope it's done soon. I don't like it when you're not around, especially at lunch."

I let the barb slide. "I know," I placated her and adjusted the pillow behind her head, leaving dirty fingerprints on the fabric.

"Is that boy still here?" she asked.

I nodded, glancing at the clock. "He'll be leaving soon."

"You'll lock up the garage, won't you, love?"

"Of course," I said with a sigh and headed back outside.

Jess laughed when he saw me. "You were worried he'd be pissed that you were talking with me, eh?" He sounded pleased.

"Would you like it if your girlfriend was hanging out with some guy all day?" I retorted. I pulled a tarp over the boxes that I hadn't sorted through yet.

"Don't have a girlfriend."

"No kidding," I said sarcastically. "Can you tarp those boxes?" I threw him an irritated glance. He watched me with a satisfied grin, as if he'd won an argument.

"Look, Rich is a really good guy."

"Oh!" he said and slapped his forehead. "*That's* why you were hiding in the garage."

"It's complicated."

"Not really. You like hanging out with me and don't want Wienerboy to find out."

I wanted to defend Rich, explain to this cocky boy that Rich would do anything for me, that his family treated me like a daughter. The "arrogance" Jess ridiculed was just Rich protecting me, making sure I didn't get hurt. But I didn't say any of those things because part of me knew Jess was right.

CHAPTER 10

JESS'S MOM WASN'T HOME YET. He kicked his shoes off at the door and flopped onto the couch. From where he lay, Jess could see down the hallway that led to the galley-style kitchen and the two bedrooms at the back. All the windows were open and a fan had been left running, but the trailer was still hot. He'd forgotten to close the blinds this morning and the sun had poured in all day.

It was Tuesday, Bingo Day on Deep River. His mom and kokum would both be there until late. His mom went to bingo almost every night, driving from town to town. He used to go with her when he was little. She'd let him eat a whole bag of Cheezies while he watched her dabber fly over the cards. He'd use his fingers, stained glow-in-the-dark orange, to paint on the cinderblock walls of the bingo hall. Once he turned eight, she'd let him stay at home alone and he'd watch cartoons till she got back. The trailer would be dark, with only the eerie blue glow of the TV flashing against his face. She was at bingo the first time he'd found her matches.

He'd wondered if he could zip the wooden stick across the cardboard and make the same scratching noise she did. It had been an experiment at first. And he'd done it! The match blazed to life in his fingers. In his eight-year-old excitement, he'd dropped it on the floor. The flame wavered and then glowed brighter. He'd stomped it out with his shoe, but it had singed a black ring in the carpet. He'd hidden the matchbook under his bed and dumped a can of Coke on the floor, hoping the stain would distract his mother from the hole.

A small mat covered the spot now.

Swinging his legs off the couch, he sat up. No point in sitting around. He'd rather be out at the river fishing than lying around the stuffy trailer. He grabbed his rod and tackle box out from under the trailer and wished he'd taken the minnows from Kokum's freezer. Maybe he could dig for some night crawlers in the riverbank. He usually got lucky in the rich dark soil under the birch tree.

A group of guys on bikes rode toward him. Tom, Rufus and Dustin skidded to a stop in front of him, pushing a cloud of dust in his face. "You doin' your service again?" Tom said it like a question even though it was a statement.

"Yep." He walked between their bikes, barely breaking his stride, but wishing the cops hadn't taken his when he'd been busted for the last fire.

"She got anything good, like something we could steal?"

Jess stopped and turned around. "She's an old, sick lady. She's got nothing. You gonna start stealing now? In Edelburg?" He gave them a cold stare. The Mounties would be breathing down his neck in a heartbeat if anything went missing from Sara Jean's house.

Tom slowly cycled around him, eyeing him like a stalking cat. "You could pocket something small. Y'know, something like jewelry, and we could sell it."

Jess shook his head at him and kept walking. "I'm not in her house, dumb-ass. I'm clearing shit out of a garage."

Tom stopped his bike in Jess's path. He met him eye to eye and kept his voice low. "My brother says some guys want to start some action on Deep River. They're gonna need some help, know what I mean? If we get a line on it now, there's nobody else they're gonna go to. Help me out, man. Just get something so's we can show we got some cred, eh?"

Jess cracked his neck. Action on Deep River. This was how it started. The gangs made in-roads selling liquor and drugs, and then before you knew it, they controlled the band and had the chief in their back pocket. Tom was as smart as a sack of hammers, but it didn't matter. All a gang needed was one guy to be the go-between, and they'd be set.

"Why do you wanna bring that shit to Deep River? It's not bad enough?"

"They're comin' anyway. Want to set up a cookhouse nearby."

Jess stared at the spotty whiskers on Tom's chin and the yellow, broken teeth in his mouth. Jess was disgusted and didn't try to hide it.

Tom stood on his pedals, making him a foot taller, and sneered at Jess. "You're such a white-boy pussy. Maybe you like hanging out with the old rich white lady, eh? Wanna be her little half-breed lover, eh? When her wrinkled titties don't make you hard no more, you'll come crawling back, I know it." He whistled for the other two and they pedalled away.

Kokum was going to be pissed when Jess told her about gangs coming to Deep River. She'd get quiet and then narrow her eyes at him, letting her chin jut forward. If she was really upset, she'd go red, like boiling anger ready to explode. She'd shake her head and go out back to sit on her stump. He never knew what happened when she sat there, but by the time she came inside, her face would be back to normal.

Someone had dumped an old mattress in the brush on the way to the river. He stopped and looked at it. A metal spring had gouged its way through the stained fabric. His fingers itched at the sight of it. He imagined the flame taking a bite of it at the bottom corner and then chewing its way through to the top until the whole thing was engulfed. He took a deep breath to steady himself, his heart quickening with anticipation.

The dry, brittle grass snapped under his feet, and he knew lighting a fire here was too dangerous. The whole field would go up. He walked away from the mattress and concentrated on getting to the river, where the cool water would wash away thoughts of flames biting their way through his frustration.

CHAPTER 11

After saying good-bye to the physiotherapist, I collapsed onto a kitchen chair and stared at the clock. Three o'clock. Rich was picking me up in two hours for dinner at his parents' place. I had to shower, return the library books and make something for Gam to eat. Another day with no time to write.

A strangled, phlegmy cough sounded from Gam's room. "Sara Jean?" she called. Bolting out of the chair, I rushed down the hall.

"Are you okay?" I asked and propped an arm behind her for leverage, trying to keep her upright.

"Fine, love, just a cough." She fell back against the pillow, exhausted from physio and the effort of sitting. After a few moments of laboured breathing, she asked, "How's the garage?"

I bit my lip, wondering if I should tell Gam everything that Jess had told me about the residential school.

"Good. We got a lot cleaned out. A few more days and it should be empty." I hesitated. "I found out some more things about that school Grandpa taught at."

"Oh." She inhaled. "That school." She said *school* like it was something dirty that shouldn't be touched. "He thought he could help those children."

I tilted my head, waiting for Gam to continue.

"They came from all over, even from the north, to live at the school and learn English. Some of them never went home in all the years they lived there. Can you imagine being six years old and not seeing your family for years?"

I could imagine. I knew the ache that stayed when a parent left.

"Some of the children did well and picked up the language and the rules, but others..." She shook her head at the memory. "They caused him no end of misery. Running away and lying and speaking their language, refusing to learn English. He had a terrible time with some of them." Another fit of coughing stopped her, and her eyes watered as she hacked away.

"I'll get you some water." I let the water run until it was icy cold. It was already three fifteen. Rich didn't like being late, especially for his parents. But I wanted to hear about the residential school so I could prove to Jess that my grandpa had tried to help, not hurt the students.

"Thanks, love," Gam said as she took the glass from me. "I hope I'm not coming down with something."

I nodded and sat on her bed.

"Is that why Grandpa left? Because of the students?"

"Oh no, nothing like that. Your grandpa got on well with children, even the ones who misbehaved. It was just" – she paused and cleared her throat – "something happened that made it impossible for him to teach there."

"What happened?"

Gam shook her head and put a hand on her chest. She grimaced in the fake way she does when a relative is visiting and she wants them to leave. "Love, aren't you going to the Wiens' for dinner?"

"Yeah." I frowned. Gam definitely knew more about the school. Why, after all these years, wouldn't she talk about it? "Do you mind if I reheat Mim's casserole from last night?"

"That's fine, love. Tell Rich's parents I said hello."

"I will." I was halfway out the door when she called me back.

"The specialist called to make an appointment. Can you mark it down on your calendar? It's for October twelfth."

My breath caught in my throat. It was the first time a date had come up that I might not be around for. I should tell her, blurt it out that I wanted to go to university. I hesitated in the doorway. Could I be that cruel? Leaving for university while she lay trapped in her bed?

Mim knew, so it was just a matter of days before she let it slip to Gam, accidentally or on purpose. Gam looked at me, waiting for an answer, smiling like a cherub.

What was the point of upsetting her before I'd made a final decision? I didn't know for sure if I even wanted to go to Winnipeg. University might not be for me, with pretentious city kids and arrogant professors. Maybe I was better off staying in Edelburg, looking after Gam and marrying Rich.

"Yeah, I'll mark it down."

"Thank you, love." She sank into the pillow, contented, while I rushed into the kitchen to put the casserole in the microwave.

CHAPTER 12

KOKUM HAD VISITORS. Two elders sat in her kitchen drinking coffee. The sugar bowl and a jar of whitener sat in the middle of the table. All three turned to the door when Jess walked in, but no one acknowledged him. Jess helped himself to coffee. It was strong and bitter. He took a seat beside Kokum. She clucked at him to be quiet as he scraped his chair on the floor.

"We probably got no choice," said Louis. His eyes were sharp and darted from face to face.

The other man, Victor Bear, puckered his lips and tapped on the ceramic handle of his mug. He took a deep breath in. "Chief got to speak for the people. You gonna talk to him, Alba? He listens to you."

Kokum clicked her tongue and shook her head. "Got to call a band meeting, eh? Let everyone have their say. Boney'll want to speak too."

"School will go. That whole bend will be underwater."

Kokum's expression didn't change, but Louis raised an eyebrow and nodded. "'Bout time."

Jess tried to follow the conversation but had no idea what was going on. Before he could ask any questions, the two men pushed their chairs back and nodded at Kokum. "See ya, Jess," Victor said.

"What's going on?" he asked as Kokum tidied the table. She motioned for Jess to put away the sugar and whitener.

"Been hearing rumours for a while now 'bout the government

trying to dam up the river. Looks like it's gonna happen. They want to put in a hydro plant and need the council to agree."

"Think it'll happen?"

She shrugged. "Don't know. Hydro will give the band a lot of money."

"You think Chief will agree?"

Again, she shrugged, turning down the corners of her thick lips. "Lot of land'll get flooded. And no more fishing. Big changes for a lot of people. Don't know what'll happen."

"When Victor said the school, did he mean the residential school?"

Kokum stuck out her lip and nodded. He knew she didn't want to talk about it and he didn't press her. Funny how the school had come up twice in one day.

"You stayin' for dinner?" she asked. "I'll fry up your fish."

"Yeah."

A kid rode by on a bike, taunting a dog with a stick. Just when the dog trotted over to take it, the kid rode ahead, keeping the stick out of the dog's reach.

He thought about the Deep River boys, what they'd told him that afternoon. He wasn't a snitch, but it made heat rise up the back of his neck. His grandmother needed to know. "Kokum, there's something else."

Drying her hands on a dishtowel, she sat beside him. Her eyes flickered over his face as she let him talk.

When he was done, she frowned. "Young people got to choose what kind of a life they want. Nothing Chief can do if the young people give in."

"But if the gangs start working out of Deep River, they'll start dealing, doing initiations. It won't take long before they run the reserve. They'll start bribing Chief." Jess felt like the weight of the future was on his shoulders. Deep River wasn't a rich reserve, but it wasn't as poor as some. He wished Tom had never told him about the gang. He didn't want to think about what it meant if they claimed Deep River as territory.

"If Hydro builds a dam, they'll build a gathering centre like on Qu'appelle Reserve. Give us money to bring back the language and teach young people the old ways. Tell Tom to come talk to me. If he wants to be a leader, there's a better way."

"I'll tell him." Jess nodded, but he knew Tom. The guy thought being a thug was the same thing as being a leader. "You ever get worried about how things change? Does it feel like they're getting worse?"

Kokum sucked in her cheeks and peered at him. "There's always bad times, no matter where you are. Lots of good on Deep River too, Jess."

Jess snorted. "Where?"

She grabbed his hand in hers. The dish soap had left her skin dry. Her boney knuckles and bulging veins felt like a topographical map under his fingers. She brought Jess's hand to his own chest and stared at him.

"I get it." He sighed, and she dropped his hand. Jess stood up. "Just wish it was easier."

She shrugged and shuffled back to the sink to finish washing the dishes. "Be good to have ice cream after dinner."

Jess smiled. "You want me to pick some up?"

"Good idea."

The wind chimes tinkled as he opened the door. From the porch, Jess could see a hawk circling. It soared and swooped overhead and then dove like a missile only to land gently on the branch of a dead oak tree. Stripped of leaves, the tree made a perfect lookout for prey. Jess waited for another minute, watching it hunt.

As he walked around the back of Kokum's house, past her window, Jess did his customary wave. But she wasn't at the sink any more. She was kneeling under the statue of Mary, her mouth working silently in prayer.

CHAPTER 13

Rich's TRUCK, NEWLY WASHED AND SHINING obscenely white in the sun, stopped in front of the house. He got out and walked to the porch, but before he could knock, I opened the front door, ready for dinner at his parents'.

"How was golfing?" I asked as we headed for the truck.

"My putting sucked. I need to get on the green more." There was a strange tension in his voice.

"Are you okay?"

His Adam's apple bobbed when he swallowed. "I've been thinking about it and I don't want that guy working at your house any more. It's not safe."

An immediate flush of heat spread up my neck. Tilting the air-conditioner vent, I let it blow directly on my face. "You'll have to talk to Gam. She put in the request for help." I tried to keep my voice calm. "I'm sure she'd love it if you did the work," I said, trying to tease him into good humour, but my voice sounded tinny and fake. Only a few hours ago, I'd been hiding in the garage with Jess, praying Rich wouldn't find me.

He scoffed. "Yeah, right. I'm not cleaning up that mess."

"So what's wrong with letting him do it?"

"I just told you. I don't trust him." Rich gunned the engine and barely stopped at an intersection.

"What do you think he's going to do? He's working in the garage." I folded my arms across my chest.

Rich shook his head at me. "He's a criminal, that's why he's got community service. It's not safe for you and Gam to have him around."

I wanted the conversation to be over. I wasn't going to tell Jess to leave because Rich wanted me to. "Maybe you should take me home. I don't want to have dinner with your parents if we're arguing," I said and looked out the window.

Instantly, Rich softened. "We aren't arguing." He pried my hand out from under my elbow and held it. "We'll talk about it later, okay?"

The drive to his parents' house took only a few minutes, like anywhere in Edelburg. A few kids were out riding bikes, otherwise it was pretty quiet. On a hot summer night like this, most people were inside basking in the cool of an air-conditioner.

Rich's parents have the biggest, oldest house in town. Built in the 1930s, it has a veranda that stretches around three sides and ornate columns on either side of the door. There's even a white picket fence around the front yard, with a little gate that Rich could step over if he wanted but that he bends down to unlatch.

Before Rich opened the front door for me, the smells of another five-star dinner wafted out. Mrs. Wiens cooks like an Iron Chef, whipping up four-course meals complete with homemade bread.

Everything my family lacked, Rich's had: siblings, laughter, noise, activity. We'd only been dating a few weeks when I got invited to Sunday dinner and birthday parties. My first Christmas at their house, I had a stocking with my name on it over the fireplace, nestled beside Rich's as if it had always been there.

Questions about our future had become a favourite dinner-time conversation topic for his sisters. Now that I'd graduated, they wanted to know when Rich was going to pop the question. Was I going to get a job? Did I want kids right away? Rich would smile at me across the table, enjoying the attention.

Mrs. Wiens wiped her hands on a quilted calico apron as she emerged from the kitchen. "Sara Jean." She wrapped her arms around me and squeezed. "Isn't this heat ridiculous? I feel like a limp dishrag."

She looked great, as usual, her hair cut in a short bob and not a smudge in her pink lipstick.

My back stiffened. No matter how often I came for dinner, I still felt like I had to impress them. A polite, forced smile plastered itself across my face. It would stay there all evening until the muscles in my cheeks ached. "Something smells delicious. Can I help with anything?" I asked as we walked into the kitchen and Rich and his dad went to the family room to watch sports.

"How's Gam?"

"Fine, she says hello." I glanced at Rich. He was smiling contentedly, our argument forgotten. This was the life he wanted: a big-screen TV and a wife cooking in the kitchen. Nodding and smiling as Mrs. Wiens related her grandchildren's latest comic exploits, I went about my chores robotically, trying not to feel stifled as I imagined myself in this life.

Mr. Wiens carried the roast into the dining room with his chest puffed up and set it down beside the carving knives at his spot. We all bowed our heads as he said grace in a deep, resonant voice. "Amen," we chorused when he was finished.

"So, Sara Jean, what's new?" Mr. Wiens asked as he passed the platter of roast beef to me.

I took the heavy plate with two hands and held it for Mrs. Wiens. "Not much –"

Rich interrupted me. "You've been cleaning out the garage."

Startled that he'd mentioned it at the table, I started to explain. "Not really me –"

Mr. Wiens cut me off, smiling. "Well, get on over there and help her out, Rich! I can spare you for a few hours at work."

"Yes, Rich. You should be helping," Mrs. Wiens admonished as she spooned corn onto her husband's plate.

"She's already got help."

Please don't embarrass me, I pleaded with my eyes. His parents looked to me, and a blush rose to my cheeks.

"It's sort of a community service thing. A social worker asked if we needed help with anything," I mumbled into my plate.

"Community service," Rich snorted. "Some kid from the reserve. What did he do anyway?" Rich asked me.

"I don't know," I lied. "I haven't talked to him."

Rich was getting more agitated. His words became short and choppy. "I told Sara Jean I didn't want her around him." He looked to his parents for agreement. I felt like a five-year-old getting scolded.

"The Indian we had working at the dealership," Mr. Wiens started, dabbing the corner of his mouth with his napkin and leaning back in his chair, "was quiet, mopped the floors, buffed up the cars. Came to work one day with alcohol on his breath." Mr. Wiens shook his head. "Had to let him go. Typical. They have no work ethic." Mr. Wiens picked up his fork and took a bite. He tented his hands and looked at his family. "They've been given everything, never had to work for a thing. Land, education, jobs. Well, heck, we even built a whole school for them and they complained about that!" Little bits of chewed meat flew from his mouth as he spoke.

Mrs. Wiens laid a hand on his arm. "Walter," she murmured.

"It's true! My tax money spent educating those ingrates, and look at them! Still drinking, unemployed and living off the system. Makes me sick." He rammed another piece of meat in his mouth and chewed it quickly, as if he was punishing it.

"That school was never a good idea," Mrs. Wiens said.

Relief flooded over me. Finally, someone with a conscience! I smiled in encouragement.

"They shouldn't have built it so close to town, not with the diseases they carried. They are not a clean people." She grimaced.

Rich laughed loudly. "If that kid starts doing a rain dance, even Sara Jean will send him packing, right?" He turned to me and waited. I felt his keyed-up energy and the pressure to react properly. Meeting his eyes, I nodded and hoped he'd drop it.

"I heard talk from one of my customers that Hydro wants to build a dam on the river," Mr. Wiens said. "But it's on reserve land, so they need the Indians to agree. You should hear all the demands they're making." He pushed his body away from the table. "New homes, community centres, money. Ridiculous! Those people have milked the system for too long."

Rich and Mrs. Wiens both nodded as Mr. Wiens continued his rant.

I'd been hoping that people in town had never known about what had gone on at the residential school, that they'd been unaware. But, as I listened to Rich and his parents, I realized I'd been dead wrong.

CHAPTER 14

THE RESERVE IS QUIET AT NIGHT. Not much traffic goes down the streets because the gas station and convenience store are closed. Jess felt like he was the last one still awake as he walked down the gravel road to his mom's trailer. The air, hot and still, smelled like Manitoba summer: sour and sweet at the same time.

The headlights of a pickup bounced on the road toward him. The truck slowed down and stopped. He coughed as it kicked up a dust cloud around him, sending stones skittering into the ditch.

"Hey, kid!" The driver leaned out of the window. Jess saw a meaty arm covered in tattoos. "You know where we can find Tom Deerchild?"

Jess looked at the truck. Kind of a beater, but not in bad shape. He walked toward it. "Who's looking?"

The driver smirked at him. His head was shaved bald. He put a cigarette to his lips and took a drag. The tip glowed orange. "You a fucking smart ass? What do you care? You know where he's at or not?"

Another guy sitting shotgun leaned forward and stared at Jess. It was too dark to see his face, but Jess didn't like the odds if he pissed these guys off. "Uh, you could ask at the gas station. He hangs out there sometimes."

The driver didn't say anything, put the truck into gear and peeled off.

Jess quickened his pace, rubber-soled sneakers grinding into the gravel road, and then decided to jog home. Once those guys discovered the gas station was closed and the reserve was quiet, they might come looking for him again.

Lights were on in the trailer when he got home, sweaty and breathing hard. He hadn't run in a long time, but it had felt good. His heart pumped and his breath came in raspy gasps.

"Jess?" his mom called from her room at the back.

"Yeah." He stuck his mouth under the faucet and drank.

His mom emerged from her bedroom and lay down on the couch.

"Hey, sweetie. You go to your kokum's for dinner?"

He nodded, sat on a chair and pulled his shoes off. They were coated in dust from the road.

"Did you hear about the hydro dam? Some guys at the diner were talking about it."

He looked up at her in surprise. "Yeah?" News spread fast on Deep River.

"They're gonna be hiring. You should check it out. Be good money." Stubbing out her cigarette, she turned to look at him and wrinkled her nose. "You run home? You're all sweaty." She slid open the pack of smokes, took one out and tapped it on the back before putting it in her mouth and lighting it.

"Yeah." He sniffed under his arms and, not smelling anything offensive, flopped on the chair across from his mom. "Kokum told me about the dam. You think it's a good idea?"

She frowned, the wrinkles in her forehead deepening. "Yeah, why not? It's Deep River, it couldn't get any worse." She took a deep puff on her cigarette.

"Kokum said Hydro's gonna pay for stuff, like a gathering centre. It'll flood the land though, and wreck the river."

"She's always worrying about something. The dam's coming whether she likes it or not. Government's not going to listen to a bunch of Indians." She exhaled, and a cloud of smoke caught the fan's current and swirled up to the ceiling.

She turned on the TV. She only had one photo of herself as a kid. It had been taken at a cousin's wedding up north, where she was born. Her and two sisters standing together in pastel-coloured dresses and poodle perms outside a church. A few years later she'd gone to Winnipeg, hitchhiking with a trucker who left her at a bus depot with a black eye and split lip.

His mom had met his dad a few weeks after she moved to the city. She said he was like her protector, looking out for her and helping her find places to eat. When she got pregnant, he agreed to take her home to the reserve where they'd be safe. His mom never talked about why she'd stayed, but Jess knew it was for him. She wanted him to know what it was like to be near family. Maybe she hoped his dad would come back one day.

Looking at her now, he wondered if this was the life she'd have predicted for herself when she left her home at seventeen. With frizzy hair and smoker's teeth, she looked older than thirty-five. Her face softened when she looked at Jess, and he saw flashes of the younger version of his mom. It made him sad to think she'd chosen this life, a trailer and a dead-end job to keep him closer to the only family he had.

If he went out west, would she stay in the trailer park? They'd lived in the no-man's land between the reserve and Edelburg since he was four years old. Their neighbours were like them, a mix of First Nations and Metis, people who didn't have status and couldn't live on the reserve but wanted to stay close to family who did.

She could get a job at a diner anywhere. Nothing kept her here but him.

"Kokum also said the old residential school would get flooded."

His mom shrugged.

"Did Dad ever talk about going there? To the residential school?"

She shook her head and blew a stream of smoke out the side of her mouth, angling it away from Jess. "Used to have nightmares sometimes. When he woke up, he said it was about the school, but never told me anything else. You could ask Kokum, she'd know."

"Don't think she likes to talk about it."

"God, no," she sighed.

"Night."

"Going to bed? Gimme a kiss." She held her cigarette off the side and held her cheek up for him. Oil from the fryer had scarred her a few years ago; pink puckered skin dotted her face. Jess leaned over and pressed his nose against hers, like he'd done as a little boy. She held his face in her hands for a moment, the butt of the cigarette touching his ear. "Love you," she whispered.

Jess didn't say anything but pressed a little harder.

CHAPTER 15

AFTER DUMPING A YEAR'S WORTH of old bank statements into the garbage pile, I pulled the next box closer to me. Gritty with dirt, the flap sent a puff of dust in the air when I opened it.

I stared in surprise at what lay on top. A pair of moccasins, small enough for a child. The nubuck coloured hide was still bright and soft, the bottoms unworn. They still smelled warm and earthy. A fringe circled each ankle and an intricate design of flowers and leaves decorated the tops. "Jess?"

He emerged from the garage. Shirtless. I'd stopped making comments, tired of feeling prudish. He dropped a stack of boxes at my feet.

"Look." I held the moccasins up, like a prize, and the beads sparkled.

"What else is in there?" he asked, prompting me to turn back to the box. I pulled out a few books and a paper folded onto itself so many times that it was a tidy package.

The ink had faded into the thick paper, and it crackled with age as I opened it. I moved into the light to read it:

Dear Mother,

I am looking after my brother, like you asked. Sometimes he cries at night, but real quiet, so the nuns can't hear him. I miss your cooking and the smell of your stew. Now that I am in my fourth year, I get to play hockey when the river freezes.

I know you can't read this letter because it is in English, but maybe the priest can read it to you.

From, your son

I wrinkled my brows and read the letter again, wondering why it never got to the boy's mother. "Why does Grandpa have these things?" I muttered.

Jess pinched his mouth tight. "He probably took 'em from some kid at the school."

"You don't know that," I said defensively.

But, after reading about residential schools online, I wasn't so sure. Survivors' first-hand accounts had been shocking: beaten for speaking their language, tied up in the boiler room for stealing food from the kitchen, forced to eat the same gruel night after night – even if they'd vomited it up.

How could anyone be so cruel to a child? I was convinced Grandpa had left after a year because he couldn't tolerate the mistreatment of the children. But why had he kept these things? The photos and the attendance ledger. They must have meant something to him.

Jess, his mouth tight, held his hand out for the moccasins. "Kokum makes moccasins like these," he said as he examined them. His eyes turned dark as he ran his fingers over the small stitches that held them together, and a frown furrowed his brow. "Everything from home got taken away from the kids."

"What should we do with them?" I asked when he handed them back to me.

"Put 'em in the garbage pile." A deerfly settled on his shoulder. He jerked his arm when it bit and slapped it away.

"We can't just toss them!" I looked at the intricate beading and soft suede. They were so beautiful. "You should show them to your grandmother. Maybe she knows who made them," I suggested.

Jess shook his head, snorting in disgust. "No one on Deep River wants to be reminded of that school."

Questions froze on the tip of my tongue as he turned away. We'd opened Pandora's box and now there was no going back. Grandpa had saved the moccasins for a reason. I wanted to know what it was.

CHAPTER 16

Jess IMAGINED WHAT IT WOULD LOOK LIKE engulfed in flames. He'd start with the far corner of the garage and watch as the fire stretched like the tendrils of a vine toward the roof. The dry wood would crack and pop, and in the end, a skeleton of the garage would be left, blackened and broken, just a picked-over carcass. His fingers itched. All day, he'd been thinking about it. Maybe he should just give in now, go somewhere closer to the reserve and light a small brush fire.

But the problem wasn't the temptation of the garage. Talk of the residential school, the moccasins, had resurrected memories of his father, memories he wished he could keep buried.

As soon as he'd held the moccasins in his hands, he knew Kokum had made them. Her signature leaf design, the beaded tendrils, one for each of her children, curled out from the centre flower. The pair Jess wore when he was a child had looked the same.

So why did Sara Jean's grandfather have them? The question burned in his mind, singeing the edges of his thoughts.

"Hey, Jess," a voice whisper-called to him from the poplar windbreak. "Jess!"

"Who is it?" He walked toward the trees, through tall, straw-like grass.

"It's me." Tom Deerchild appeared. He had a cut on his forehead and a fat lip. The rest of his face looked puffy, already red and blue and about to turn purplish.

"Shit. What happened?" Jess took a wide stance. He didn't want Tom getting too close to Sara Jean's house. Better he stay hidden in the trees.

"Some guys came to find me last night. From the city."

Jess winced. "How'd they find you?"

"Just knocked on someone's door. Said they were visiting. Took me out for a drive and left me a couple miles away."

"Fuck! I told you this would happen!" Jess wanted to punch something. Adrenaline rushed through him. "Why the hell do you want to get mixed up with those guys?"

Tom looked like he might cry. Hanging his head, he couldn't speak.

"What do they want you to do?" Jess balled his fists and steadied his voice. He didn't want Sara Jean to come outside. He didn't want to see her expression when she saw some kid from the reserve with a messed-up face.

"They want to deal on the reserve. Cook out at the old school."

A meth kitchen. Jess swore again. If Tom had been closer, he would have hit him. "You brought this shit here, Tom. You clean it up." Jess was ready to walk away, but turned back. "Wait. Tell 'em about the new hydro dam. There's going to be Mounties and government pricks all over the place. No way starting up now is a good idea."

"We're getting a dam?"

"Soon as Chief agrees."

Tom nodded his head, his eyes wild and scared, like a hunted deer. "Okay, I'm gonna do it. You gonna back me up though, right? I can let 'em come to you if they don't believe me."

Jess ran a hand through his hair. "Why do I gotta get mixed up in your shit? Just go tell 'em." Tom backed away and had almost disappeared when Jess called to him. "Don't ever show your boney ass near here again!"

Jess looked around, wondering if any of Sara Jean's neighbours had seen Tom.

How could Tom be so stupid? What did he think would happen if he invited gangs to Deep River? If the hydro dam didn't go through, the gang would be back. They might be back anyway, not caring about some white guys hanging around. He wanted to tell Kokum, but what could she do? She was right, the change had to come from the young people now. It was up to Jess and his friends. The thought sent a fireball to his gut.

Cracking his knuckles, he felt the familiar itching and fidgeting in his fingers return. *Just one small dumpster fire*, he promised himself. He needed to gain control of the situation and that was the only way he knew how.

CHAPTER 17

TOOK THE MOCCASINS INSIDE when I went to check on Gam. They'd upset Jess, but that wasn't enough reason to throw them away. As I hid them under my bed along with the note, the photos and the school ledger, I realized I'd have to do my own digging to find the answers.

We worked quietly after lunch. I carefully sifted through each box Jess carried over, and the pile grew.

"Supposed to be a storm later," Jess said.

"Really?" I asked, throwing him a look and gesturing to the sky. A few marshmallow clouds dotted its blueness. The air was humid, though, and even with my hair up in a ponytail, I could feel the dampness on my neck.

"I'm part Indian. Don't argue with me about the weather. He gave me a lopsided smile, lifting the tension, our argument forgotten. "Best time to fish is right before a storm."

"Why?"

He shrugged. "Dunno. The fish sense the change or something."

"Must be nice down by the water," I said thoughtfully, picking through a box of *LIFE* magazines from the '80s.

"It is. You should come with me." It was a challenge. He dropped the box he was carrying and looked at me. "How could you live here your whole life and never go fishing?"

I looked at the never-ending piles of boxes and felt my heart sink. The heat and dust clung to me. Going inside the house meant giving Gam a full report, and even if I made it upstairs to my computer, I was too distracted to write.

Rich wouldn't like it, me going fishing with Jess. In fact, I couldn't believe I was even considering it. But dinner at his parents' had left a bitter taste in my mouth. The thought of doing something daringly out of character was tantalizing.

Jess heaved an impatient sigh and threw tarps over the boxes. "Soon as everything's covered, I'm heading out. You can come if you want to."

The smart thing, the proper thing, would be to say no. But I was tired of doing things that way. It was time to take a leap. "Should I bring sandwiches?" I asked.

Jess grinned at me and my stomach lurched. "No mayo on mine."

The air conditioner barely made a difference in the house. Just slapping mustard on bread, I was sweating.

"Gam?" She was sleeping again. She'd been sleeping a lot the last few days. Probably the heat. "Gam?" I used my whole weight to shake her awake. Her skin felt clammy under my fingers.

She stirred and looked at me, bleary eyed. "Robyn?"

I caught my breath. She'd never called me by my mom's name before. "Gam, it's me, Sara Jean." I sat down on her bed. "Are you okay?" There were dark circles under her eyes.

"Sorry, love. I must have been dreaming."

"About Mom?"

"I can't remember now." Gam's voice drifted off.

"I'm going out for a while. Mim will be here soon for lunch. Do you need anything before I go?"

Gam looked at me as if I was abandoning her. "You're coming back, though?"

A flash of edginess stirred in me. When had I ever not come back? Her tether on me only let me go so far.

"Yeah, of course. I'll be back in a couple of hours."

"Where are you going?" she asked, her forehead wrinkling.

I sighed. "Out." I couldn't tell her where, or with whom.

"You don't usually go out during the day."

Because I'm stuck here with you, I wanted to remind her, but of course I didn't.

"What time will you be back?"

"Gam!" I cried, exasperated. "I don't know! And it's none of your business anyway!"

She recoiled with a look of astonishment.

Taking a deep breath, I adjusted a fan so it would circulate air over her face. Wisps of stringy hair flew across her pillow, the odour of her body dissipating.

"It's hot out, and I'm tired. I didn't mean to yell," I explained. Guilt made my chest ache. "Do you want anything before I go?"

She stared at me reproachfully. "I feel a little light-headed," she said. "Maybe a glass of water?"

I nodded and went to the kitchen. From the window, I saw Jess waiting beside the car, holding Grandpa's old rods.

The water refused the get cold. After a few minutes, I gave up and let it gush into a glass. I took it to Gam, but she'd fallen asleep, her breathing deep and even. Mim would be here soon. I took a final glance at her and left.

The car rattled to life; I barely drove it, relying on Rich and his ever-changing chain of pickup trucks, each one bigger and better than the last. Jess blasted the air conditioning and rolled down the windows, but it didn't make a difference. The suffocating heat of the car made it hard to breathe. I tossed the sandwiches in the back.

"You know where the trailer park is? I need to stop at my mom's to pick up some bait."

I nodded and reversed out of our property. If anyone saw us, I had a story ready. Jess had heat stroke and needed to get home. Totally believable. I glanced at him from the corner of my eye. His face was turned to me, and his eyes were closed. The hollow of his throat was shiny with sweat. *It isn't right for me to be looking at him*, I thought. Gripping the steering wheel tighter, I turned my eyes to the road.

CHAPTER 18

THE PRAIRIE GRASSLAND SPREAD FOR MILES on both sides. People often joked that you could see your dog run away for three days. Jess knew the road by memory, the hills and dips, curves and farms. A stand of trees up ahead guarded the river-bank, and he could see the one-lane bridge that crossed the river. Somewhere along the road, his fingers had stopped itching for the first time all day. Tom's visit had shaken him. How would he ever be able to leave with guys like Tom hanging around, making stupid decisions?

Sara Jean pulled the car off the road and parked in the shade of the trees. They grabbed the rods and bait from the trunk and slammed it shut. A few birds, startled by the noise, burst from the trees.

The slope to the river was steep and slippery with loose pebbles. Jess worried Sara Jean would fall in her flip-flops. He held out his hand to her. She hesitated and then took it.

The river had carved out the bank beneath, so the land hung, unbalanced, over the water, a veil of exposed roots reaching for the river. Jess jumped down to the pebbled shore. He watched as Sara Jean estimated the length of the drop and waved away his hand. She walked to the edge, sat down and slid off, landing beside him. The sun filtered through the rippling water, the colour of the river stones shifting like a kaleidoscope.

"It's pretty here," Sara Jean sighed, gazing across the river where a thicker forest stood. "Peaceful."

He'd started to knot a lure on her line. A sinker was asking for trouble; here, the river was too shallow. He'd be tugging gooey seaweed off her line all day.

"Can I ask you a question?"

Jess looked up.

"Was this the first time you got caught?" she asked quietly.

At first he didn't know what she was talking about. But as she stared awkwardly at her feet and bit her lip as if she regretted the question, he figured it out.

He'd never told anyone about the fires. He thought of them like his garden; each fire was like a plant that came to life and bloomed in front of him. His shoulders tensed and he was about to bite back, make a nasty comment that would stop her from asking questions.

She looked up, and her blue eyes, innocent and curious, met his. He shook his head slowly and went back to tying on her hook.

Sara Jean took a deep breath and sighed. "Why do you do it?"

Jess shrugged, wondering how it would feel to say it out loud. "I don't want to set them. But it's like if I *don't* do it, something worse will happen. Watching something burn means I've saved a different bad thing from happening." He knew it sounded crazy, but maybe she'd understand because there was hurt inside of her too.

"Do you feel better? After you set them?"

A breeze blew tendrils of hair from her ponytail. The heat wasn't as oppressive now that they were by the water.

"For a while. I feel calmer. But it doesn't last."

She slid her shoes off and stretched out her legs. He laid her rod down and picked up his, searching in his tackle box for a jig and a lure.

"You come out here a lot?" Sara Jean leaned back and closed her eyes against the heat of the sun. Jess's eyes lingered over the curves of her body.

He held the line in his teeth as he tied a knot and mumbled,

"As much as I can." He gave a wry laugh, "It's the only good thing about living here." He looked out over the river, with its sunlit ripples and gentle current. "For now, at least. If they build a dam, this'll be a dead lake."

The serene look on Sara Jean's face disappeared. "What do you mean?"

"No current. The fish die. All this" – he gestured to the land around them – "will be flooded."

She stared down the choppy, flowing river. Birds chirped and the water slapped the rocks.

"No more fishing," he said.

"So much for the one good thing," Sara Jean muttered.

"If the dam goes through, it'll be a good time to leave." He shrugged. "See what else is out there, you know?"

"Yeah." Sara Jean bit her lip and pulled her knees up under her chin. "I got accepted to U of M. I could start in September," she said.

Jess made a noise in his throat, a soft murmur of approval. "You gonna go?"

"I don't know. I'm worried about leaving Gam. And telling Rich," she admitted. "And I'm scared." Her mouth was set in a thin line, as if she was disappointed in herself.

"There's always a reason to stay. I guess there has to be better reasons to go."

She considered this. "Staying means giving in. I'll end up with Rich and looking after Gam forever." Her eyebrows wrinkled together. "Maybe that's why my mom left. She knew if she didn't, she'd be stuck here forever with me."

"You think she was right to leave?"

"No." Sara Jean bit her lip.

Jess could see the pulse in her neck throbbing.

"I think she should have been stronger and stayed. I wouldn't ditch out on someone who needed me."

Jess snorted. "Guess that's why you're having trouble figuring out if you should go to school, eh?"

"Hmmm." She gave a wry smile. "Guess so."

"I think my dad left because he thought it would be better. Didn't want me to see him as a drunk, y'know? Better to ditch out than be a shitty father." Jess cast his line in one fluid motion, the hook kissing the water and sinking underneath. He turned to Sara Jean. "Guess I better show you what to do. Not much of a teacher."

She gave him a half-smile as he reeled in his line and laid the rod down between them. "Put your hands here," he instructed, "and then pull the rod back and flick and release when you want to cast the line."

She pressed her lips together, concentrating on getting it right. Her first casts ended with the hook swinging off the end, like a tetherball, when she forgot to take her finger off the release.

Sara Jean squealed on her third try when the hook landed in the water several metres away. "Now what?"

Jess grinned at her. "Now we wait. If you feel a tug on the line, start reeling it in."

Reeds on the other side rustled when a muskrat slithered into the water and dove under. The muskrat reappeared, his brown head slick and shiny, a silvery fish clutched in his mouth. *Show off*, Jess thought.

"Jess!" Sara Jean gasped as her line went taut. He put down his rod and moved closer.

"Reel it in slowly, that's right." Her line was probably stuck on the bottom, nothing was fighting on the end of it, but Jess liked watching as her cheeks flushed with excitement. "Keep going." Sara Jean's rod curved down the water as she kept turning the reel, her face intense. When the line loosened, she fell back, her hook bouncing out of the water. A silvery fish arced out of the river, chasing the lure. Its tail whipped past them as it caught hold and pulled the line back down with it.

"Keep reeling!" Jess shouted.

Sara Jean grabbed the rod but forgot to turn the reel as more line went out. "What do I do?" she screamed.

"Keep reeling!" Jess said again and moved behind her, putting her hands on the spinner. "There you go," he said. The weight on the end of the line pulled her toward the water. "Stand up. Don't let it win, you have to tease it up to the surface," Jess coached her. The tendons in her arms strained as she used all her strength to hold the rod.

"There it is!" Jess could see the silvery scales flashing under the surface. "I'll grab your line as soon as you reel it out of the water, okay?"

Sara Jean nodded, too focused to speak. Suddenly, the fish burst from the surface, fighting and thrashing to get back in. Jess waded into the river, the cool water swirling around his ankles. He grabbed for the line and held it still for Sara Jean, who had rivulets of sweat running down her face. Carrying it to the shore, he put the fish down on the rocks. The gills flapped as if water still ran through them, and tiny teeth were visible through its mouth.

Sara Jean stared at it, her eyes shining and her cheeks glowing. "What do we do with it?" She laughed.

"Throw it back." Jess took out the hook and held it up by its gills, careful not to let the teeth bite him. "It's a pike, no good for eating."

"Really?"

"But look at it. This fish is a fighter. Big too."

Her face lit up at his compliment. "I'm shaking! I thought it was going to yank my arm off."

"Here." Jess handed the fish off to her. Sara Jean recoiled, but he insisted. "Throw it back in." She tried to grab it around its middle, but Jess laughed. "You have to hook your finger through the gills, like this."

Tentatively, she reached out a finger and slid it between the gills as Jess took his finger away. She carried it at arm's length and walked to the river. There was no pungent, fishy smell; it wasn't dead yet. This fish smelled like the river, the plants and the stones. Each metallic scale shimmered like an oil slick. "Now what?" she asked.

"Let it go."

Taking a deep breath, Sara Jean bent down. As soon as the fish's tail touched the water, it squirmed, flapping back to life. Sliding her finger out, she let it drop to the water. It didn't move at first, but as the water coursed over its gills, it sprang to life and swam away, reborn.

CHAPTER 19

"**W**E SHOULD GET BACK. Clouds look ugly."

I turned around, surprised to see a bank of purple storm clouds hovering over the field. The breeze had died down and the air sat still and heavy. "Yeah, guess so."

"You did good," Jess said with a smile.

"Thanks." I wondered if he felt the same rush every time he caught a fish, or if it was so normal for him, the feeling had been lost. "How do we get up?" I asked, staring at the high, eroded bank.

He put his hand on my back and propelled me toward an exposed tree root. "Grab on. I'll help you." I threw my flip-flops up first and, using the roots, hauled myself up. My already exhausted arms felt like jelly by the time I clawed my way onto the grassy hill.

Jess tossed the fishing rods and tackle box up and, in one graceful leap, appeared beside me, grinning. The clouds hung low in the sky, purple-grey and ominous.

"We should hurry," I told him as he picked up the rods and tackle box. The car was close by, but driving country roads in a thunder storm, with rain pummelling the gravel, wasn't fun, especially in my old car.

"Race you!" I called, laughing as I got a head start. Even with the gear, Jess caught up to me. I pulled out one final burst of speed and slapped the hood of the car a second before he did.

"I let you win." He grinned.

"You did not," I giggled, surprised to hear the high-pitched, giddy laugh come from my mouth.

"You don't think I could beat you in a running race?"

"Nope," I answered with a shake of my head. Catching the fish, sitting by the river, being away from Edelburg, something had left me feeling euphoric.

Dropping the rods and tackle box, he rubbed his hands together and crouched in a runner's stance. "To the tree. Ready?"

I kicked off my flip-flops again and lined up my feet with his. "Go!" Pumping my arms, I could hear Jess breathing beside me, short puffs of air as he pulled ahead. Determined not be beat, I pushed my legs, willed them to move faster and harder. My feet slapped the ground, toes crushing the grass and springing forward.

Jess touched it first, but my hand was only a second behind his, the satiny birch bark smooth under my fingertips. A laugh burst from my lips as I stood panting. Jess bent down to catch his breath. "You're fast," he said between breaths.

"Long legs," I gasped.

The clouds hovered over us now, obliterating the sun. It would only be minutes before the rain came. "Come on," I said, grabbing his arm. "We better go." At that moment, it would have been natural for him to put his arm around me or even kiss me. We were both laughing and relaxed. I wanted him to. I could feel my body aching for his attention.

A lump formed in my throat. What kind of a girl did this to her boyfriend? A liar and a cheater. But that couldn't be me. I was a sweet, innocent girl from Edelburg. As I watched Jess saunter to the car, a hint of a playful smile on his lips, I realized that maybe I wasn't.

DROPS OF RAIN EXPLODED AGAINST ME as I raced in through the back door. It had come down hard as soon as I'd dropped Jess off at his trailer, smattering the windows and exploding against the windshield. Shaking the rain off, I noticed how muddy I was. My hands and knees were filthy. I needed a shower. A smile lingered on my face as I walked into the kitchen. My annoyance with Gam before I'd left was forgotten. I wished I could tell her I'd caught a fish, but then I'd have to explain what I was doing by the river.

As I walked farther into the house, I could hear voices, men's voices. What was going on?

Tearing through the kitchen, I collided with Mim. She shrieked, as startled as I was, but past her I saw a flash of navy pants. Who was in my house?

"Where were you?" she hissed. I turned to her, stunned. Did she know I'd gone with Jess? Had she seen me?

"What do you mean?"

Her talon-like fingers grabbed my arm.

I looked at Gam's room. There were two people in there dressed in white shirts and dark pants. A stethoscope hung from the neck of one. My chest heaved and my head swirled. "Gam!" I shouted, fighting Mim's grip. "Gam!" I raced into Gam's room. Plastic tubes were attached to her nose and arm. Machines in suitcases lay scattered on the floor and an oxygen tank hissed. "Gam?" My voice trembled.

"She's still unstable." The female paramedic looked up from her kit. "We're trying to arrange transport." *Oh God*. The wind sucked out of me, like a vacuum, and my knees buckled. I tried to grab the bed for support, but missed and crumpled to the floor.

"Miss? Are you okay?" The other medic took my arm and led me to the chair. It felt solid against my rubbery legs.

"Mim?" I called out weakly, like a child. "Mim?"

A flash of Gam before I'd left her, disoriented, calling out to Robyn, a thin layer of sweat on her pale face. Now it made sense. She'd probably been having a heart attack while I stood in the room with her. And instead of staying, I'd yelled at her and gone off with Jess. A burning numbness rose up my neck. The room started to go fuzzy.

Mim gripped my arm and pulled me to my feet. She dragged me out of Gam's room and into the hallway. From the door, I stared at Gam's inert body, plugged into so many machines it looked like they were growing out of her,

"What happened?" I asked, my voice cracking.

"She was convulsing when I got here. I called 911, and thank God it wasn't too late." She shook her head. "Where were you?"

Sobbing, I shook my head. The truth was too horrible to say. I wanted to throw up knowing what I'd let happen.

Gam stirred. The plastic tubes made turning her head difficult. The EMT leaned over her. "Ma'am? Can you hear me? Alice?"

Gam nodded her head weakly, and her eyelids fluttered.

"Gam?" I choked on my words and rushed to her side. "I'm so sorry, Gam! I'm so sorry." She moved her fingers as if to pat my arm, and I reached for them to assure myself of their warmth. Mim bustled in and pushed me aside.

"I'm here, Alice. Do you want something?"

Her head wobbled slightly side to side, and she closed her eyes again.

The female EMT stood in front of me, her face free of judgement. "Her heart was in A-fib when we got here and not pumping blood properly. We gave her oxygen and medication, but we can't get a regular rhythm."

Mim interjected. "Dr. Kehler's meeting us at the hospital."

A voice buzzed through their radio with instructions. Two more men arrived, and the four of them slid Gam off her bed and onto a gurney. Her sides hung over the edges, like her body was dripping off.

"Sara Jean?" Rich's voice filled the space between me and Gam. He reached for my shoulders and I melted into him, grateful that he was here. "Is she okay?"

I shook my head and started to cry. What was he doing here? Had Mim called him?

"It'll be okay." He patted the back of my head like I was a child. "Where were you? Mim called me, looking for you."

My body shook with sobs and I pressed my face against his shirt, muffling my lies. "Nevermind. Don't worry about it."

Pushing himself away, he looked at me. "Why is there mud on your face?"

My face went crimson. "I was outside." *Not a lie*, I told myself, trying to keep an invisible tally.

"Go clean up and I'll take you to the hospital."

They'd wheeled Gam down a makeshift plywood ramp to the waiting ambulance. It shone slick with rainwater. They'd pulled a tarp over Gam's body, and one held an umbrella over her head while I watched from the doorway. All four of them grunted with effort as they pushed her up another ramp and into the ambulance. Mim hopped in after, but they shook their heads at her. Not enough room. I didn't offer her a ride with Rich and me.

CHAPTER 20

JESS RAISED AN EYEBROW at his mom's frenzied cleaning. She'd pulled out the carpet broom and was huffing as she ran it across the carpet. The bristles were so short and compacted that usually a stiff broom swept away the crumbs and dirt. All the blinds had been pushed back, and the usual layer of dust on the windows had been wiped away and replaced with the smell of ammonia cleaner. The rain had started to come down hard, pummelling the packed dirt outside.

His mom pointed to the small coffee table, and he lifted it so she could vacuum underneath it. She usually worked the breakfast and lunch shifts at the diner. What was she doing home? "You okay?"

She stopped the vacuum and blew a piece of hair off her face. With one hand resting on her hip, she examined the trailer. "Yeah. Destiny needs tomorrow off, so she's working for me today and I'll do a double tomorrow."

"What's with all the cleaning?" Jess flopped down on the couch. Even the two velour pillows had been placed neatly in the corners.

She shrugged but pressed her lips together as if she was containing a smile. "You hungry? I got Hamburger Helper."

Jess narrowed his eyes at her. "No. Ma, what's going on?"

"Why? Cuz I'm cleaning?" she hooted. "Pretty sad when watching your mom clean freaks you out." Shaking her head, she stuffed the vacuum into a tiny closet beside the bathroom.

"Kokum wants you to go over."

"She say why?"

"No." Percussive thumps of rain rattled the windows.

"Can I go after the rain stops?"

His mom shrugged. "Up to you."

He turned on the TV and watched as his mom sorted through a junk drawer and put away dishes. "Saw Tom Deerchild today. He looked rough. Said he fell off a quad."

Jess snorted. A quad? "Where'd you see him?"

"Over at your kokum's."

Jess muted the TV, his hackles raised. "What was he doing over there?" It wasn't unusual for his mom to go to Kokum's for a cup of coffee on her day off. But Tom?

"Don't know. He ran off when I got there."

"What did Kokum say?"

She paused in her tidying and looked at Jess. "Why? Something going on?"

Jess put his feet on the floor and rested his head in his hands. Why was Tom dragging Kokum into this? "He played with fire and got burned." His mom cast a sharp glance at him. "He got roughed up. Offered a gang something he couldn't deliver."

"Shit." His mom slammed the drawer and the cutlery jangled.

Jess grunted in agreement.

She eyed him warily. "You're already on community service. You stir up trouble..." She let her voice trail off. Jess knew he was only months away from getting tried as an adult. He jumped up from the couch and strode across the room in a few steps.

"I'm going to Kokum's." Jess grabbed a rain jacket and pulled up the hood. His rubber boots were tucked under the trailer. As he stuffed his feet into them, a fork of lightning seared the sky. He only counted to five before he heard thunder. Swearing as he ducked into the downpour, he took off to his grandmother's.

She stood by the stove, warming up soup. The aroma of salty chicken broth flavoured the air.

"Shoulda waited till it stopped," she told him as he hung his dripping jacket on the hook by the door.

Jess shrugged. He didn't tell her his stomach had been in knots the whole way over. Was Tom using Kokum to get to him? How desperate was he to get the gang off his back?

He sat down at the kitchen table, sticky, cold and sweating all at the same time. A mug of warm broth appeared in front of him.

"Got some news," she stated and sat down across from him, putting her elbows on the table.

Jess slurped the broth and set the mug down. "Mom said Tom was here."

"That's not the news."

He waited. Heat from the mug seeped into his fingers.

"Got word from your dad. He wants to come back."

Kokum watched him, unblinking. Her nostrils flared in and out as she breathed. Jess felt like he'd been turned to stone.

For once, she did the talking. "He's sick." She looked at her hands, the colour of dried oak leaves. "Friend offered to drive him home."

Jess snorted at the word *home*. He didn't belong here any more. "No."

"Not asking you."

"I won't see him." Jess stood up quickly and his chair tipped over. In three strides he was at the door, pulling on the wet rain jacket. Without saying good-bye to Kokum, he slammed the door and took off in the downpour.

Cleaning the trailer! He sneered. Even after all these years, his mom was still trying to play house with the guy who'd ditched them. His dad had balls to come back now. Jess's fingers started to itch. He pressed them together hard in the pocket of the jacket, trying to make them numb.

He was almost home when he remembered why he'd gone

to Kokum's in the first place: Tom. Veering toward the river, he took an overgrown path back to the reserve. A canopy of trees protected it from the rain, and dry kindling sticks cracked under his feet. Gangs, the dam, his dad, a lot of shit to deal with. His breath came in short bursts, but he clenched his jaw to keep the emotions buried.

The scratch of a match igniting.

Heady scent of sulphur.

Sizzle and flare as the flame took.

Crackling heat as the fire grew.

Jess leaned against a tree and tried to steady his breath. The pull to set something on fire was overwhelming, like a thunderstorm rolling over him, and he felt powerless.

CHAPTER 21

I HATE THE COLOURS THEY PAINT HOSPITALS. As if the dusty pinks and sea-foam greens distract anyone from the fact that they are in the hospital. Those colours are cursed, forever associated with illness and worry.

A fluorescent light flickered, the tube buzzing with strangled energy. Gam was on her gurney nearby. She was awake now, after the ambulance ride, and uncomfortable. Away from her bedroom, she didn't look like Gam any more. Nurses and aides walked by. Some did a double take or stared outright. I wanted to shield Gam from them, take her away from this place.

A man came and wheeled Gam into a room where we had to wait until more aides could be found to help move her. Mim went to get tea. Bleached white scratchy sheets the thickness of cardboard lay on the bed. How long would Gam need to be in here? A wave of nausea hit me at the thought of being separated from her.

"You okay?" Rich looked at me with concern.

I nodded. Part of me wished he'd leave. I didn't deserve his kindness.

Gam stayed silent when they moved her, her eyes wide and frightened. The bed was big enough, thank goodness, and her mass expanded to fit it.

"Gam, do you need anything?"

She shook her head, but tears leaked out the sides.

"Gam! I'm so sorry. I wasn't gone for long. I knew Mim was coming so I didn't think… I'm so sorry, Gam." I buried my face in her shoulder and sobbed pleas for her to understand.

"Sara Jean," Gam wheezed and stroked my head with her hand. The oxygen tube got tangled in her fingers. Smiling through my tears, I sat up to help her.

"I'm going to wait outside," Rich said and closed the door. It was just Gam and me.

"You're my angel, love." Gam looked at me with such adoration, my heart ached.

A shaky breath. "I wasn't there. I should have been there."

She closed her eyes, as if the words hurt her. "I need you to do something for me."

I nodded. *Anything.*

"You have to find your mother."

The rhythmic beep of the heart monitor filled the room. I stared at Gam. "How can I? She doesn't want us."

Gam shook her head almost imperceptibly. "It was me. I made her leave." Another tear rolled from the corner of her eye.

"What? What do you mean?"

Gam made noises in her throat, as if the words were stuck. "I did it for you." She took a tremulous breath, meeting my eyes. "To spare you. All the shame. Of being born that way." Each word came out slowly, painfully. Her nostrils flared defiantly, daring me to argue.

Moving away from the bed, I stared at Gam, trying to make sense of what she was saying. My mom hadn't left because she didn't want to be a mother? She left because Gam was ashamed of her? The room started to drip away, like a watercolour painting. Things came in and out of focus.

Gam loved me, why would she do this?

"Sara Jean." She reached out a hand to me. "Come here."

I shook my head and stayed where I was, out of her reach.

"You need to find her. Tell her to come home."

Breath stuck in my chest, like I was suffocating under the pressure of her request. Gam was asking me to do what I'd have died to do all the years I was growing up.

Mim walked in. She froze holding two Styrofoam cups of tea. Her eyes flicked from Gam to me. "What?" She looked to Gam.

Gam turned her head to face the wall. Mim put the tea down on the bedside table and glowered at me. "What did you do?"

A derisive laugh escaped from my lips. "What did *I* do?" I narrowed my eyes at her. "What did *I* do?" Pushing past her, I stormed from the room, not even pausing for Rich. He jumped up from the hallway chair and jogged to catch up with me.

"What happened?" he asked.

"Take me home, okay?"

He opened the door to the truck for me, and I got in. Balled-up energy coursed through me. I couldn't speak, or even think. I willed the tears to stay away until I got home as we drove silently through town.

"Do you want me to come in with you?" he asked when we pulled up to my house.

I shook my head. "No."

Rich kept a hand on the wheel, but turned off the truck. "You seem pretty shaken up. You sure?"

"Yeah," I said, unbuckling my seat belt.

"Sara Jean." He grabbed my hand. I took a deep breath. He squeezed my fingers. "Why don't you come to my house for dinner tonight?"

The idea was so preposterous, so exactly opposite of what I wanted to do, I laughed. "What?"

Rich stared at me, confused.

"No." Exhaustion overwhelmed me. Walking up the front steps looked like an insurmountable task. I made it and opened the door without saying thank you or good-bye.

The house was silent. Of course it was. I was the only one home. I'd never been the only one home – ever.

I'd been left with nothing. Gam had lied to me my whole life. She'd taken my mother from me, and now she wanted me to find her.

Thoughts muddled themselves in my head. I spun around in the hallway, not knowing where to go, feeling lost in my own home. Was this what freedom was like? Sleep. I wanted to sleep. I stumbled up the stairs, fell onto my bed, kicked off my shoes and hoped that when I woke, something would make sense again.

CHAPTER 22

TOM LIVED BESIDE THE RIVER. Seven people, give or take, in a two-bedroom home. In the summer, he set up a tent and slept outside. Jess could see the dark green tent through the trees. The shouts of children inside the house filled the yard with noise. One of them burst through the door and leapt down the front steps, racing past Jess in a whirl of shirtless energy. Two more took off after him, and a dog barked, trying to get in on the chase.

Jess walked in without knocking. Tom, his dad and a few uncles were gathered around the kitchen table. A couple of empties sat in the middle of it and general disorder was everywhere. Toys, pillows, clothes were strewn across the dirty floor. Holes had been punched in the walls in a few spots, and kids had coloured or left muddy handprints in other places. The place smelled moldy and damp.

"Jess." Tom's dad eyed him and pushed a chair out with his foot. "How's it going?"

Jess ignored the invitation of a chair and caught Tom's eye. "Need to talk to you," he said and jerked his chin to the door. Tom hesitated, but pushed his chair away from the table and followed.

"Why'd you go visit my kokum?" Jess snarled in Tom's face.

Tom's nostrils flared, but he didn't back away. The cut on his face had swelled and scabbed over.

"Told *you* to handle it," Jess said.

Tom rolled his shoulders like a boxer before a match. Jess saw him wince. The pain from his beating was evident. "Thought about what you said. About telling them to leave." He pushed past Jess and leaned against the porch railing. "But then I was thinking, why the hell am I listening to a fucking half-breed, eh?" His lips curled up in a sneer. "This place is going to shit anyway." He eyed Jess. "Never gonna get Hydro here. You're lying, trying to make excuses." Tom had always been an asshole, but this was a new side of him, as if he had nothing to lose.

Jess ran a hand through his hair, trying to keep his cool. "You're a fucking idiot –"

Tom cut him off, pointing a finger in his chest. "The only reason you're here is your gran. Once she goes…"

Jess's knuckles caught him on the chin with a wicked blow that brought him to his knees, one arm hanging over the railing, as his body collapsed to the porch. He staggered up, holding his face. Jess's chest heaved with shallow breaths, his fist balled, ready to throw another punch.

Tom's dad burst from the house. He'd been a drinker all his life and his belly swayed ponderously under a dirty grey T-shirt. The porch shook with his weight and sudden movement. "What the hell?" he shouted.

Jess didn't explain. He gave Tom a murderous look and jumped down the steps.

"He's fucking nuts, Dad. Crazy like his old man!"

Jess wanted to finish the fight, go back and feel bones cracking under his fist, but it was suicide. Tom, his dad and the rest of them would tear him apart. He ducked back into the bush, droplets from the leaves shaking off as he walked.

When he got to his mom's, he saw that all the lights were out. She must have gone to bingo. Jess stood at the door and waited. Some music from a trailer nearby floated through the air, but otherwise it was quiet. He walked to the bush behind the trailer and rolled a boulder over. Under it, in a hole he'd dug, lay a box holding a few rags, bottles and matches. Sometimes he wished the box would be empty. And other times he smiled in relief.

Tonight, he was just checking, reassuring himself that if he needed them, they were there.

CHAPTER 23

I'D NEVER WOKEN UP IN AN EMPTY HOUSE. Without the sound of Gam's strained breathing or television chatter, I was aware of every noise I made: the flap of the covers as I pushed them off me, the creak of the bed as I sat up. It was early, and the sky glowed pink and orange with broken clouds lining the horizon.

I felt older as I stared around my room, as if I'd aged overnight, no longer innocent Sara Jean. The protective glass around me had cracked. How could I go back and face Gam?

I had so many questions. Had my mom gone willingly? Had her departure been dramatic? Preceded by a fight? What biting words had Gam said to convince her to leave me?

And Mim. She would have known. Why had she kept it a secret from me?

There were still three hours before the hospital allowed visitors. Maybe by the time I went to see Gam, my head wouldn't feel so blurry. I shuffled downstairs and put some water on to boil. I needed to write. Not my book, there was too much buzzing for that, but a letter to my mom. Even though I'd probably never send it, releasing the ideas trapped in my head might clear it. Things would make sense.

I carried my cup of tea upstairs and turned on my computer. A new, blank page appeared, and I sighed. Bearing down, I wiggled my fingers and narrowed my eyes. Do I write *Dear Mom* or *Dear Robyn*?

Dear Mom, I began and stared at the screen. What next?

I've spent the last seventeen years of my life thinking you didn't want anything to do with me. I know now that's not true.

Gam is sick. She had a heart attack and is in the hospital. She asked me to find you and tell you. I wonder if you even care after all this time? If you do, you know where to find us. It must be weird to get a letter from me. There is so much I want to tell you. I hope you come back.

Sara Jean

What if she had a husband and kids of her own? This letter might be a reminder of her shameful past, a life she tried to forget.

Should I try to find her? I didn't even know where to start. I'd searched for her online before, typing in her name, but nothing had ever come up. Maybe she had a new last name or had moved far away.

I didn't know if I could face Gam, my emotions were so jumbled, but I needed answers to the questions swirling in my head.

MACHINES BEEPED AND HUMMED in her room when I walked in. The door shut behind me on cushioned springs with barely a sound. Gam was asleep, hooked up to monitors, but breathing normally. Light shone in through slits in the vertical blinds, illuminating slivers of bland paintings and metal medical equipment. Gam's body odour was masked by bleach and alcohol, but faintly present and familiar. A nurse padded in silently on rubber-soled shoes. "Are you family?" she asked.

"She's my grandma."

The nurse nodded, smiling.

She checked the IV. Gam stirred and murmured something

unintelligible. I stayed off to the side, watching. The nurse was middle aged, with gold earrings and pink lipstick. Her arms were thin and veiny. She looked miniature next to Gam, who was three times her size.

"We'll be waking her up for breakfast in a few minutes, anyway," the nurse said as she left.

"Gam?" I whispered. "Gam, it's me."

"Wha – oh, Sara Jean." Gam sounded surprised. She blinked as if she couldn't believe I was there. The sheets rustled under her as she moved to face me. She opened her mouth to speak, but nothing came out.

"How did you sleep?" I asked, trying to sound normal.

She gave me a weak smile that didn't reach her eyes. "Not very well. All these cords and tubes and beeping. And this bed, it's not like home."

"Did the doctors say when you'll be able to leave?"

"They want to make sure the medication is working. It might be a few days." She pursed her mouth, making her cheeks dimple. "Sara Jean." Her voice dropped to a whisper. "I need to talk to you about Robyn."

I leaned in.

"When I told her to leave, it wasn't – well, it wasn't because I didn't love her. I did, of course. She was my daughter." The words left her in strangled gasps, as if they were being pulled from her throat against her will. "It was always to protect you, love."

I frowned. *To protect me? From what?* Pangs of unwanted hostility toward Gam flashed through me.

She took a deep, shaky breath, as if telling the truth caused her pain. "Your mother lives in Winnipeg. Her name is Robyn Delcourte now." I stared at her in shock. "She has two other children, a boy and a girl."

I gasped. Her words like needles, piercing.

Gam reached for my arm, but I pulled it away.

"No!" I stood up and backed away from her. She'd robbed me of a brother and sister, of growing up as part of a real family.

How dare she ask anything of me when she'd taken away so much?

"You have to know –" she started and broke off, gasping. The machine beside me began to beep and flash. Gam fell back against the pillow, her back arching.

I watched soundlessly as she flailed in her bed, choking. Nurses rushed past me and crowded around the bed, shouting words and hauling equipment closer to her. In front of my eyes, her gown was off and electric paddles jolted her body. She convulsed, but the beeping kept going. The nurse I'd met a few minutes before looked up at me. "You need to leave. Now!" she commanded. I felt like a zombie, moving to the door, not feeling its weight as I pushed it open or the glare of the light in the hallway. A doctor ran toward me, stethoscope flapping against his chest. "What have we got?" I heard him yell before the door shut, muffling their voices.

I stood alone in the hallway as Gam took her last few breaths on the other side of the door.

CHAPTER 24

THE STORM HAD CUT THE HUMIDITY. Jess didn't wake up damp with sweat like he had for the past week. Today was a fishing day. A day to dangle a line in the water and lounge on the riverbank, not really caring if anything bit, and jumping in to cool off when the sun got hot. Maybe Sara Jean would go with him. The thought made him smile. He liked being with her. She was awkward and quiet and she'd picked Wienerboy as a boyfriend, but she made him feel better.

But when he arrived at her house it was quiet, and the car was gone. A note had been taped to the garage door. "At the hospital with Gam." He'd get to fish after all.

The sound of a car stopping in front of the house made Jess turn back. As he walked around the garage, he saw the gleaming white pickup.

"Don't think she's home," Jess called as Rich got out of his truck.

Rich puffed up his chest and checked to see if the car was gone. He ignored Jess.

"She okay? The old lady?"

With one foot on the running board, Rich turned to him. "None of your goddamned business."

"Tell Sara Jean I'll wait for her. The garage is gonna take longer than I thought, maybe weeks." Jess let a taunting smile spread over his face and waited for a reaction.

Rich stepped down and came toward him. He was a few

inches shorter and scrawny, but his lips curled in distaste and a nasty glow shone in his eyes. Jess took a step back. "Stay the fuck away from her, you filthy son of a bitch. Your kind doesn't belong in this town and never has. And you sure as hell don't belong around my girlfriend."

Jess raised an eyebrow. "That's not what she thinks." Jess knew Rich would run at him before the words left his mouth. Bending his head like a battering ram, Rich charged and hit Jess in the chest. But Jess was ready and caught him under the arms, flipped him over and raised his knee into Rich's lower back. Rich yelped and Jess let go, backing away and waiting for Rich to come at him again. Getting to his feet, Rich spit on the ground. He smoothed his hair and straightened his shirt, his breath coming in short bursts.

"That's it? That's all you got? *Pffft.*" Jess waved at him like he was a pesky mutt.

Rich kicked at the gravel and a few pebbles ricocheted off Jess's legs. He walked back to the truck and got in, slamming the door.

Jess gave Rich the finger as the truck pulled out of the driveway in a flurry of spraying stones. He watched the truck until it disappeared around a corner then he went to sit by the garage. The tarp covering the boxes was dotted with puddles. He didn't want to go fishing any more. He wanted to see Sara Jean and to know she was okay. Rich was an asshole. What if he threw Jess's words back at her? He didn't want her to be blindsided.

He'd only been sitting there a few minutes when a car pulled up. A dusty blue one with shiny chrome hubcaps. It was the skinny lady whose jerky movements reminded him of a marionette: Sara Jean's Aunt Mim. She came around from the driver's side and opened the passenger door. Reaching in, she pulled out Sara Jean. Her head hung down and her arms hung limply at her sides. The woman struggled to move her.

Jess's walk changed to a trot as she yanked on Sara Jean's

arm. "Hey, what happened?"

Mim started at his sudden appearance, her hand flying to her chest. "Oh! You gave me a fright." Her eyes were swollen and red. "What are you doing here?"

"I came to work, but no one was home." He looked at Sara Jean. She'd collapsed against the seat, whimpering like she was in pain. Jess bent down and peered in. "Sara Jean? Are you okay?"

Mim butted her head between them. "Help me get her inside."

Jess pried her out of the car and kept one arm around her waist. She hung against him as silent sobs shook her body. He could feel her ribs convulsing.

"Upstairs." Mim pointed when they got inside. Sara Jean's bed was unmade, the sheets rumpled at the bottom. Setting her down as gently as he could, Jess stepped back. Mim brushed the hair off Sara Jean's face, took off her shoes and pulled the sheets up to her chin. She turned away from them, curling her legs up to her chin, and cried like she was breaking in half.

Jess looked at Mim, a question in his eyes. She nodded and pursed her lips against her own tears, which came anyway.

Bowing his head, Jess left.

CHAPTER 25

IT WAS THREE DAYS BEFORE I ATE ANYTHING and five before I left my room. Mim stayed in the spare room down the hall and came to check on me, probably often, but I don't remember. All I remember is opening my eyes and noticing if it was sunny or dark, but not caring, and then drifting back to sleep. Or whatever it was. Maybe not sleep, more like a being in limbo, a self-induced coma, until my brain could process what had happened.

By the fifth day, I took shaky steps to the window. There were noises outside, unfamiliar ones. I stayed off to the side and pulled the curtain back. An old pickup truck sat in the yard by the garage. Jess, shirtless, tossed boxes, rusty farm equipment and tools into the back of it. They clanged against each other, and sometimes the tailgate wobbled and creaked with the weight.

Letting the curtain fall back in place, I shuffled to the bed and rested my hand on the brass knob at the foot. With a deep breath, I willed myself to make it downstairs and have a piece of toast. Mim must have heard my footsteps because a minute later she was at my side, holding my hand as if I was a toddler learning to walk.

The kitchen looked the same, nothing had been changed. Some dishes sat on the drying rack in the sun, light gleaming off the washed glasses. When the toast popped up, Mim buttered it, scraping the knife against the top so it crumbed and ripped.

"He's been out there all morning." She nodded toward the garage. The quiet was broken by each thud of more boxes being piled into the truck.

I took a tentative bite of the toast. It felt foreign in my mouth. Dizzy and light-headed, I forced the rest of it down and drank some water.

Mim sat down across from me. She'd never been a maternal figure, and even now, she looked harsh.

"The funeral's today. I put it off as long as I could."

I nodded. Somewhere in the haze of the last few days, I remembered her telling me. "What time?"

"Three. Will you be okay?"

Blood drained from my face. "No. Will you?"

She raised an eyebrow in a teacherly way, calling me out on my attitude with a look. Sighing, I closed my eyes. "What time do we need to leave?"

"The Bethel Women's Group at the church will have food ready, so we should be there a half hour before to greet people."

"Okay." I'd go on autopilot. As people came up to shake my hand or hug me, I'd give a wan smile, nod and look to the next one in line. I hoped no one showed up.

"They're expecting two hundred people."

"What?"

Mim shrugged. "Everyone loved Alice. She was very popular back in her day, active in the church and all that."

"What if I don't go?" I looked at Mim, my jaw set.

She cocked her head at me. "What do you mean? She was your grandmother, why wouldn't you go?"

I shook my head, tears welling up in my eyes. "I can't face everyone. The way they look at me."

Pinching her mouth together, she grabbed my plate and put it in the sink. "Well. That's lovely. The daughter missing and the granddaughter can't be bothered to show up."

I narrowed my eyes and stared hard at her back. "She's not missing. She's in Winnipeg."

Mim turned around. "How do you know?"

"Gam told me before –" I broke off, not trusting myself to finish the sentence. "She wanted me to find her."

Mim frowned, watching me. "What else did she tell you? Her voice changed, got softer, and her probing eyes lost their edge.

I started to sob. The memory of my last conversation with Gam was too sharp. Its edges dug into me. I'd said hateful things, and now she was gone. "My mom has other kids. And, she told me..." – hiccupping sobs made it hard to speak – "that she didn't leave because she wanted to." In a second, Mim was at my side, pressing my head against her boney chest. The plastic zipper of her windbreaker imprinted on my cheek. She knelt down and held my face in her hands.

"She loved you so much," Mim said.

The unexpected compassion made me cry harder. I didn't know if she meant Gam or my mother.

"You need a tissue," she said, wiping away a tear. I heard her rustling in Gam's room, and when she returned she had a wad of tissues but also the small wooden box where Gam kept her Bible. "Here." She opened the lid and took it out. Underneath was a packet of letters tied together with string, like a present. Mim pulled them out and handed them to me. "These are for you."

CHAPTER 26

HIS CLOTHES HUNG OFF HIM and he smelled sour, worse than a drunk, like something was festering in him. Jess could smell him from the doorway.

"Hiya, Jess." He acted like he'd just left to buy milk instead of ditching him and his mom years ago with no explanation.

Jess stayed at the door, his hands stuffed in his pockets. He didn't want to go in or get any closer than he had to. Kokum went to the cupboard and pulled out a box of cookies and set them on the table in front of the couch, trying to lure Jess inside.

"Gah, you're grown up, eh?"

Jess snorted. "That's what happens when you fuck off for five years."

His dad licked his lips, eyes darting to Kokum and back to Jess. "Yeah, guess so, eh."

"You're sick?" Jess asked, hoping his words hurt.

"That's what they tell me. Liver cancer."

"How long?"

His dad shrugged, pushing out his bottom lip. "Don't know. Wanted to come back though. Be with my people."

Jess erupted. "Your *people*? What people? You left your people with no money! No food! Nothing!" He flung his arms out. "You have no people!" He turned to go.

"Jess!" It was Kokum. She never raised her voice. "He wants to make peace. Time to listen, eh?"

Glowering, Jess kept one foot in the house, one foot outside.

Kokum levelled her gaze at him, and he moved all the way inside and shut the door.

His dad pressed his lips together and swallowed. "I know you hate me. Don't blame you. I came back to make peace with you and your mom. I didn't want to leave this world without ever making things right, eh?"

Jess looked hard at his father. Missing teeth, skin with a yellow tinge, hair that grew in greying tufts over his head – Jess searched for compassion for the man sitting across from him. His distended belly didn't match the gaunt, skeletal face.

"Haven't had a drink in a while. Had to go to the hospital, eh, and they don't serve booze on those little dinner trays. Tried to straighten out."

"What's the point? You're dying now, anyway."

Kokum stamped her foot on the floor, making the plates on the table rattle.

His dad looked at Kokum. "I didn't want to come home a drunk."

She nodded. "Gus, take Jess fishing. Show him how it's done."

Snorting, Jess turned to go. He didn't need any fatherly bonding now. He didn't even know the guy sitting on his grandmother's couch, pretending to be his dad. "I fish fine. Don't need him to show me."

Kokum ignored him and began puttering around the kitchen. Part of Jess, a big part, wanted to show his dad that he didn't need him. He'd grown up on his own, become a man while his father had been dicking around in the city. With a sigh, he glowered at his father. "Can you walk?"

"Yeah, long as we go slow."

Jess grunted his agreement and let the door slap shut behind him.

THEY WALKED IN SILENCE TO THE RIVER, Jess in front, carrying the rods and tackle box. The sun sat high in the sky and beat down on Jess's neck. He wished he'd worn a hat as he walked into a cloud of gnats. The rain had hatched a new crop of mosquitoes, and one whined in his ear.

"Guess you graduated this year, eh?"

"Yeah," Jess answered and set his chin.

"Gonna move to the city?"

"Don't know."

"Wish I'd never gone." His dad laughed mirthlessly. "An Indian can't make it in the city. Shoulda stayed here. Biggest regret I have is leaving you and your mom."

Jess rolled his eyes. "Took eight years and liver cancer to figure it out." Glad he couldn't see his dad's face, he ducked off the road and led the way on a path through some trees.

"I'm not proud of my life. Made bad choices. Let drinking take over."

Was he looking for forgiveness, making excuses like that? It had taken eight years to destroy their relationship, and it would take at least that long to repair it. Jess's breath caught in his throat when he realized his dad didn't have that long. By the looks of him, he might not even have eight weeks. They walked silently to the river, down a worn path criss-crossed with tree roots. A squirrel raced in front of them and leaped to a tree, spiralling up the trunk to a branch and chirping at them.

Jess turned to see his dad's face light up with a smile when they got to the river. "Ha! Hasn't changed." He stared at the water's eddies and ripples and took a deep breath. "Gah, that smells good. Like fish and mud, eh? Don't smell that in the city." He picked a long piece of grass and held it between his hands and put it to his mouth. A high-pitched whistle sounded as he blew.

Jess remembered his dad trying to teach him how to do that when he was a kid. His warm, dry hands cupped over Jess's as they sat in the tall grass.

"What d'you got for bait?" his dad asked. He went to the edge of the river and stood looking over it with his hands on his hips, as if he were the Creator surveying his work. Jess walked beside him and stuffed the container of night crawlers he'd taken from Kokum's freezer into his distended stomach.

His dad, unfazed by Jess's rudeness, held them up like a prize. "I remember digging for these when I was a kid, eh? We'd sell 'em to Loeppky's for a penny a worm." He hooted at the memory. "Then he'd sell 'em for ten cents."

Jess could feel his nostrils flaring. He didn't want to be here. He didn't want to hear about his dad's happy childhood memories. This whole outing was bullshit, concocted by Kokum to what, help them heal? He wanted to laugh at the absurdity of the idea.

His hook poked through the rubbery worm, making it convulse and contract. Jess took a few steps away and cast. His line sailed through the air and landed in the middle of the river.

"Nice," his dad said.

Jess ignored him.

"I stopped treatment to come out here. Don't have much time left, but I've made my peace with that."

Did he want an award? Jess steeled his jaw and stared at the line. A pressure at the back of his throat made it hard to swallow.

"I'd hate me too, if I was you, that's for sure."

Jess looked at him out of the corner of his eye. His shaking hands made it impossible for him to bait the hook. He looked worn out and exhausted, like a popped tire; there was no buoyancy left in him. Jess reeled in and set his rod on the pebbles at his feet.

He took the worm from his dad's hands and pressed the hook into it, feeling the resistance of its innards. As he handed it back to his dad, their eyes met. The chasm between them was so deep, so filled with years of pain and hurt, that it might never be bridged.

His dad sniffed and stood up, wobbling a little. His first

clumsy cast didn't go anywhere. But, after a few tries, muscle memory kicked in and his line floated through the air.

His body relaxed as he pulled on his line, testing it, letting some out and reeling it back in. "Ma said you come here a lot, that you're pretty good."

Jess shrugged, pleased that his grandma had said those things. "Guess so."

"My dad taught me to fish. Used to fish at the school. The nuns would let me out of class so I could catch dinner. Used to catch enough to feed all the kids." The line grew taut and he spun the reel. "Rock," he said when the line released.

His dad cast his line, the hook slipping soundlessly into the water and drifting downstream. "Kept me out of trouble, being the best fisherman."

Jess didn't say anything and reeled in his line, preparing to cast again. As he bent down to pick up another worm, he heard a sharp intake of breath from his dad. His shoulders tensed as the rod bent and went slack, teasing a fish to the surface. With an explosion of water, the silver-scaled fish burst to the surface, its body contorting in mid-air. Jess stood waiting with the net and lunged for it before it could fly off the hook.

It was seven pounds at least. The fish flapped in the net, coiling itself in the strings until it lay still, its gills taking final fluttering gasps.

Charged with energy, his dad slapped a hand on Jess's shoulder. "Beauty! Ma's gonna be happy, eh. Prove to her I haven't lost the Indian in me," he said laughing.

Jess sat down and pulled the hook out of the fish's mouth. The tang of fresh fish lingered in the air. His dad sat down beside him with his arms resting over bent knees, winded but exhilarated. Suddenly, he was wiping away tears, his shoulders shaking. Jess looked at him, annoyed. He didn't want to see his father cry. He inched away and stared across the river.

With a shuddering sigh, his dad took a deep breath and shook his head. "Didn't realize how much I missed this place."

He stared out over the river. "Took me a long time to get up the guts to come back."

Jess clenched his jaw against all the things he wanted to say.

"Meetings helped. Always thought those AA people talked a bunch of bullshit, but once I started going, I saw. Us Indians, we all got the same story. Same pain. From the schools."

Jess waited for him to continue. The fish lay on a rock in the sun. Some flies, glistening like oil slicks, feasted on the new catch.

"Took me a long time to figure it out. How I got this way." He looked at Jess. The whites of his brown eyes were tinged with yellow from the cancer, and underneath, pouchy pockets of black showed through the papery thin skin.

"Thought coming back here, I could find some peace."

A hawk dove down, enticed by the fish, its glide smooth and effortless as it soared back to the tree and gazed down on them.

"I need you to help me, Jess."

Winding a blade of grass between his fingers, Jess thought about it. He didn't owe his dad anything. He could get up and walk away, and even his kokum would understand why. He slid his thumb along the rough underside and let it unwind, leaving an unruly blade amongst the rest. He didn't say no.

The hawk flew off, no longer interested in someone else's catch.

CHAPTER 27

ALL THE PEOPLE, THE QUIET CHATTER, the hugs passed in a blur, like a car speeding by in the opposite direction. Rich stood behind me in church, his hand solid on my shoulder.

"Take me home?" I asked him, as Mim helped the ladies restore order to the church basement that always smelled like fried perogies and floor wax. Funerals, baby showers and wedding receptions had all been hosted here. I'd been in the space so often, for so many reasons, I didn't know if I should love it or hate it.

"Sure," Rich said. My dutiful boyfriend. He'd hovered over me all afternoon, refilling my glass and casting protective glances my way. Now that the funeral was over, we were both exhausted.

The house was silent. Rich stood in the entryway. "I can stay," he offered.

Shaking my head, I stood near him and leaned in for a hug. With his arms wrapped around me, I almost forgot that going forward, everything would be completely different. "Thanks for coming today."

He rubbed my back. "You don't have to thank me."

"I know, but still." I leaned back and gasped. "Did I thank your parents?"

Smiling, he said, "Yes, twice."

"Oh. Good."

"You must be tired. Why don't you get some sleep and I'll

come by tomorrow after work?"

I nodded and locked the door after him. I was officially alone. The house felt foreign, like an enemy, not comforting and familiar. As I walked to the kitchen, I looked out the window. The grassy field stretched out to the horizon line. It was a constant. Even with everything else changing, I could count on that view. The boxes were gone, an indentation on the grass the only trace of their presence.

I had a lot of decisions to make. Stay in the house? Go to school? Move to the city? The box of letters from my mom sat on the kitchen table. I could only read a few at a time before I was overcome with anger and sadness. For years, she'd been writing to me, telling me about her life and how much she missed and wanted to see me, promising the time would come when we could be together. She must have realized I never saw the letters – that Gam had kept them from me.

What was Gam afraid of? Did she think I'd choose my mom over her, or blame her for keeping us apart? Maybe the secret had gotten too big to tell, and it was easier to keep pretending.

The letters had stopped coming four years ago. Right when Gam's diabetes got bad. Had Gam told her to stop writing, or had my mom given up?

The return address was Plum St., Winnipeg. Sounded pretty. Did she live in an old house on a tree-lined street? Or in one of those new developments where the houses all looked the same? Now that I had an address, it wouldn't be hard to track her down. If I wanted to.

A knock on the back door startled me. Jess peered through the glass. My feet felt heavy as I shuffled to the door and opened it.

"Hey." His eyes softened, and he tried to smile. "Here. Kokum said it'll help. Some kind of a tea." He shrugged. "If you're having trouble sleeping."

"Thanks." I took the glass jar of dried flowers and held it in my hands. "You got rid of everything," I said, motioning to the yard.

"Yeah." He stood awkwardly, shifting from foot to foot. "I just came by to say sorry, you know, for your, uh, loss. And –" He broke off and ran a hand through his hair. "Can we go sit outside?"

I put the tea on the counter. I hadn't changed out of the uncomfortable black dress pants I'd worn to the funeral, and the wide legs flapped around my ankles. We walked to the garage and sat in the shade. "Guess it's been a shitty week for you."

I closed my eyes and nodded. "I didn't think it would hurt like this. My whole body aches, like I've been hit by a truck."

"Were you there when it happened?"

I nodded.

His arm came around my shoulder and lay there, protective and heavy. "Sorry," he whispered again.

Wiping away some tears, I shook off the emotion. I needed a break from thinking about it. "How are you? Have you been fishing or anything?" I asked.

He took his arm away and clasped his hands together. "Been fishing a little." He paused, as if he didn't know how to continue. "With my dad."

"Your dad?" I asked with disbelief.

"Yeah, he came back a few days ago. He's sick." Jess's voice sounded far away, like an echo of someone else's. "He keeps talking about making peace, whatever that means." He shifted his body so he could look me in the eyes. "Something else shitty happened this week."

I looked at him, not sure if I could handle more bad news. At least sitting beside him, I didn't feel like I'd fall to pieces. "What?"

"I finished cleaning your garage." He gave me a half-smile. "Now I got no reason to come by."

I wanted to say the house needs to be painted and the lawn mowed, but I couldn't. No matter what Jess's feelings were, I still had a boyfriend, one who'd stood beside me in church today and followed me around like a bodyguard.

Jess looked at the ground. "You don't have to say anything. I just wanted you to know. I gotta go." He stood up, dusting gravel off his shorts.

"Wait!" The strangled sound of my voice surprised me. "Can you stay, for a while?"

As he sat down, I knew I'd tell him everything about Gam and my mom and the letters.

His fingers brushed against mine tentatively. I opened my palm, welcoming the gentle pressure of his hand in mine, and closed my eyes to let the warmth of his touch sink in.

"It would never work. We could never be together," I whispered. My voice broke as I let my hand fall away. "It just wouldn't."

His eyes turned hard. He made a noise in his throat and frowned at me. "Why? Cuz I'm from the reserve?"

"No. Because we want different things."

"You don't know what you want."

"I know I don't want to be stuck here." The words flew off my tongue.

"You think I do?"

I narrowed my eyes, hoping for the same honesty I'd given. "Do you?"

He paused and gave an ironic laugh, "Actually, yeah." He looked in the distance, and I wasn't sure he was talking to me any more. "I didn't think I did, but I do."

CHAPTER 28

HIS DAD HAD BEEN HOME FOR A WEEK. Jess had discovered that he talked – a lot – and could put people at ease with a joke. Jess kept a wall up, unwilling to forgive him. But he liked how he felt when he walked around Deep River, now that his father had come home.

As dusk faded to night, and purple fringed the edge of the horizon, Jess walked beside his father to a bonfire at Kokum's sister's house. The same pickup Jess had seen a couple of weeks ago blew past them. He thought he saw Tom's face in the rearview mirror sneering at him. He followed the headlights as they turned off the road toward the residential school.

When he turned back, his dad was watching him. "What's going on?"

Jess shook his head. "Nothing."

"Why're they going that way? Nothing up there but the school."

"Don't know," Jess replied and kept his head down.

"That school should be torn down," Gus muttered under his breath. "No good ever came from it."

Jess glanced at him. In the dusk, the yellowish tinge to his father's skin wasn't noticeable, but shadows deepened the gullies in his cheeks. He wondered if the walk over had been too much for him after the day of fishing.

Kokum was already sitting at the bonfire when they got there. Dressed in a blanket coat even though it was warm out.

Her face split into a grin when she saw them through the smoke. She waved them over to sit beside her, shooing some kids out of the seats. Jess's great-aunts and uncles, cousins and family members he knew he was related to but didn't remember how, sat around the fire, swatting at mosquitoes and stabbing bonfire forks through hotdogs. Sparks flew up toward the sky as the fire twisted and snapped in the breeze.

Jess's fingers hadn't been itchy in days. Even sitting by the fire, he felt nothing but the strength of its heat, no compulsion or desire to create one of his own. He laughed as one of the little kids pulled out a wiener, charred beyond recognition, and, with an impish grin on his face, gave it to his dad to eat. Gus took it and pretended to chew it as if it was the most delicious thing he'd ever tasted.

Jess relaxed into his lawn chair, the rickety metal legs and woven plastic seat squeaking against him.

Old Boney Stephens was drinking on the far side of the circle and muttering something about the residential school. Before long, Gus threw in his two cents worth.

"At least if the dam goes through, that goddamned school will be torn down," he said, shaking his head.

"Shoulda been torn down years ago." All eyes turned to Louis, whose cheek bulged with a wad of tobacco.

Gus snorted in agreement. "I'd tear it down myself, if I could." A heavy sadness filled his face.

Old Boney cleared his throat, tapping a pointed charred stick on the edge of the rusted oil drum. Sparks flew up, spinning into the darkness. "Kids who went into that school didn't come out the same."

Kokum spoke, her voice quiet against the crackling fire. "Five kids they took from me. Gus's brother Phil died there. Never knew about it till the spring when they sent Gus home. He had to tell me." She shook her head, bitterness curling her lips.

Jess watched as his dad balled his hands into fists at the mention of Phil's death. A gust of wind blew smoke toward

Jess, making his eyes sting. He remembered the shrinking tail lights of the pickup as it turned toward the school. A lot of bad had happened there, and more was coming.

"It should be torn down," Jess said, as surprised as everyone else to hear his voice, but now that he'd started, it was too late to stop. "Some guys are turning it into a cookhouse for meth. Tom Deerchild's one of them. A gang wants in on Deep River."

The atmosphere of the bonfire changed. It had stopped being something fun and social. A knot formed in Jess's stomach as all eyes turned to him.

Kokum stared at him across the fire, rocking gently in her chair. The firelight flickered across her face.

"Tom tell you this?"

Jess nodded. "Wanted me to help him." Jess could feel his dad's eyes on him.

"Why didn't you?" he asked.

It was hard for Jess to explain, but he knew that path wasn't the one he wanted to be on. He was no angel, he had a blue file with his name as proof, but he wasn't interested in spending his life with guys like Tom.

"One more reason to tear the place down," his dad muttered.

There was a chorus of agreement. Jess's eyes swept around the campfire, taking in Boney, Louis and the others. They were old, wrinkled, with sagging jowls. *And sick*, he thought, when his eyes landed on his dad. They'd lived in the school's shadow their whole lives and done nothing about it.

He thought about the moccasins and the letter Sara Jean had found in her garage. Hidden away for forty years, they had a story to tell. The school had tied the reserve and his family together in a twisted knot. Jess looked at his father, sitting morose, probably desperate for a drink.

The time for talking was over. It was time for action.

CHAPTER 29

"**C**OME ON, I GOT A SURPRISE FOR YOU." Rich stood on my doorstep.

"Rich," I whined, "I haven't even showered."

He had that determined look on his face, and I didn't bother to argue. Since Gam had died, Rich, his parents, Mim and the neighbours thought they knew what I needed: casseroles, a good night's sleep and cookies topped the list.

I needed to be left alone.

I'd started writing again, nothing big. I didn't have the energy to tackle the book, but I wrote other things: ideas for short stories, memories of Gam, stories she'd told me about life in Edelburg when she was a girl. I'd pulled out some of Grandpa's journals, savouring the smell of old leather and the cover's worn edges, to read about him and Gam when they were younger. I could hear his voice as I turned the pages – and the laughter. I'd forgotten about the laughter and the love we shared.

Some days I'd only get through a few minutes of reading or writing before I'd be crying too hard to continue, but a lot of times I left Grandpa's office feeling lighter, as if some of the grief had been stripped away. And then Rich would show up, full of good intentions, and I'd be yanked back to the real world, the world where I had decisions to make and secrets to keep.

"Give me a minute," I sighed and ushered him in.

"You cleaned up a lot," he said, looking around. I'd moved Gam's medical equipment to the garage and pushed her bed to one side of the TV room. And I'd cleaned the room, scoured it with bleach, trying to erase the stale odour of obesity. I didn't want to remember Gam stuck in a bed, held captive by her weight. "My mom would have helped, you know?"

I paused in mid-step. His comment was typical, but today, it grated on me. I clenched my teeth together, fighting the urge to lash out at him.

"Do we really have to go somewhere?" I asked.

"Yes." He grinned, excited about whatever it was. "No arguing. Go get changed." He gave me a gentle shove toward the stairs.

I was in my room when I remembered the piece of paper on the fridge.

"Rich?" I called, bolting down the stairs. "Can you come –" Too late, he had it in his hands.

His eyes flashed to me. "What's this?" He looked hurt and confused.

Should I lie and say it was Mim's? That it was her book list because she was thinking about going back to school?

I cleared my throat and took a step closer to him. Enough lies. "My book list for university."

He cocked his head at me. "Huh?"

"I'm going to the U of M."

"Why didn't you tell me?" He didn't sound angry, just surprised.

"I thought you'd be upset. I didn't even officially decide until a few days ago."

His face broke into a grin, "No, that's great. Good timing actually."

I stared at him. This was not the reaction I'd expected. Where was the anger? The frustration at not being included in the decision?

"Come on, hurry up!" he said, pushing me out of the

kitchen. "Get dressed so we can go."

Still reeling, I threw on a T-shirt and jean cut-offs. I hadn't even shaved my legs. If the book list hadn't fazed him, some leg hair wouldn't either.

"Where are we going?" I asked, getting into his truck.

"That's the surprise." He started the car, and we drove through town. I resisted the urge to duck as we passed people on the sidewalk. Hiding out in the house was the only way I could avoid the endless condolences and sympathetic pats on the arm. I knew they meant well, but I wanted to be anonymous, move to a place where people didn't know I was grieving.

We turned onto a gravel road, in the direction of the reserve, and then veered north. There was nothing out this way except farmers' fields and, in the distance, the residential school. We'd driven about twenty kilometres on the road when Rich pulled off, his truck plowing over the golden stalks of wheat.

"Rich, what's going on?"

He laughed. "You look so freaked out! Don't worry. Close your eyes, we're almost there."

With a concerned glance at him, I kept my eyes open and waited. The truck bumped and jostled toward a grain silo, standing at attention in the middle of the field.

"Come on, get out," he said, parking the truck in front of the corrugated metal silo.

"Why?" I asked, not moving. What could he show me here? We were knee-deep in a sea of wheat.

"You're gonna like it," he sing-songed and walked around to open the door for me. It reminded me of when he'd made me play hide and seek for my computer at Christmas. Was this fun for me, or him?

Hand in hand, we walked around the silo, trampling the stalks of wheat. *What is so interesting about a silo?* I wondered. Rich stopped walking and gave me a satisfied grin. When I looked up at the silo, I choked back a gasp of surprise.

"I love you, SJ" was scrawled across it in white paint.

Rich grinned at me, enjoying my shock. "I want you to know that I'll always be here for you, no matter what happens." His voice grew earnest and serious. "And now, with you going to school, I know this is the right thing to do." Reaching into his pocket, he took a deep breath. My heart plummeted. He got down to one knee and held a box in front of him. He was actually doing this. *Oh God.* I felt dizzy. "It's not an engagement ring, not yet," – he gave me a sly grin – "but a promise ring."

Tears sprang to my eyes. He had it so wrong. Everything about this was wrong. As I was preparing to find my way out of Edelburg, he was doing everything he could to keep me here.

"Rich." My voice cracked. "I can't believe you're doing this."

His face was flushed. He looked like a shiny new apple. He was waiting for me to say yes.

"Oh." It came out like a moan, not what a boyfriend wants to hear when he's down on one knee. "Rich." I shook my head and closed my eyes. What was he thinking?

When I opened my eyes, he turned away from me and gave a bitter laugh. "Guess I'm an idiot."

"No." I took a deep breath and hoped I'd be able to explain. "I'm just not ready for this. Not yet." *Not ever.*

All the hope and tenderness had left his eyes when he faced me. "When? When will you be ready? When you've gone away to get some stupid degree to prove how smart you are?" He took a step closer. "You're alone, Sara Jean. You have no one!"

His words pierced me. They echoed in my head. *I have no one.*

"We belong together, before anything gets in the way. We'd be happy."

I have no one.

Something sparked in me. A fire ignited. I stared at him and the silly velvet box in his hand. "*You'd* be happy. I just told you how I feel." I walked toward the truck and opened the door, refusing to look at the silo. Did he really love me, or did he love the idea of me, a wife to look after, someone who owed everything to him?

He stormed around to the driver's side, tossed the ring into the glove compartment and slammed the door shut.

"I'm only eighteen. Now's not the right time," I said, trying to stay calm. But inside, I knew, it would never be the right time. Not with him.

"Lots of girls get married at your age. I'm twenty-one. My parents had already had my sister by now."

"We're not your parents."

"What's wrong with my parents? They've done pretty well for themselves."

"Nothing wrong with your parents, Rich," I sighed. "I just don't want to live in Edelburg for the rest of my life, okay?"

He shook his head. "Who looked after you after your gam died, Sara Jean? Who brought food and checked in on you? All the people you're so happy to leave behind, that's who." He put the truck into reverse and pressed hard on the gas pedal. Stones flew out from the wheels. "Fine. Go. Go to Winnipeg. I hope you find everything there that we can't give you here." His face twisted with bitterness and anger.

We drove in silence back to town, his fingers squeezing the steering wheel so hard I thought it would snap. He drove fast – dangerously fast – down the gravel roads, kicking up a cloud of dust and fishtailing around corners.

When he pulled up to my house, I waited for a minute before unbuckling, hoping he'd say something, but his mouth was wired shut.

I leaned my head against the back of the seat. "I'm sorry –" I started, but he cut me off.

"Get out."

"Rich?"

"I said, get out!" The venom in his voice frightened me. I'd never seen him so angry. I jumped out and ran into the house. When the door was locked behind me, I slid down to the floor and let the pent-up emotion flood over me. It didn't hurt like Gam's death had, but the hollowness in my chest threatened to swallow the rest of me.

I have no one.

He was right. But the words he thought could scare me into staying with him were the ones that would drive me away.

CHAPTER 30

Jess BOUNCED IN THE BACK OF THE PICKUP as it coasted over the gravel road up to the residential school. A lone silo rose up from the middle of a field. At first he thought the gang had tagged it, but as they drove closer, he saw it said, "I love you, SJ." It couldn't be. He shook his head at the irony. How'd the bastard get up that high?

When they got to the school, Jess hopped out of the back and surveyed the building: broken windows, weeds growing around the gravel yard, mortar crumbling from between the bricks. It was as run down and forgotten as its students.

"Ha-looo!" Old Boney hollered. A few crows squawked as they flew off the roof, but other than that, stillness. A few outbuildings lay in the same sad state of disrepair. Pickets on a fence were broken and crooked.

Boney and Jess's dad walked toward the building and went around to the back. Gus had started to look very frail the last few days. Jess had seen the cocktail of medicines he took each day and wondered if the magic powders inside them were keeping him alive or if it was will power. Jess walked up to the front door. Chains and a padlock held the handles together, but he yanked on it anyway. He couldn't help thinking about all the kids who had walked up these steps and how different they were when they walked out. He wondered what it was like for his father to be here after so many years.

"Jess," his dad called from behind the building, and he went to see what was up.

"Looks like that's how they're getting in," Boney told him, pointing to a broken window.

"That used to be the priest's room, right there. And the boys slept on the third floor. Nuns and girls on the second." His dad pointed to the row of windows above them. A cloud passed over his face. "Used to cry into my pillow, quiet as I could. The nuns would beat you if they heard."

Jess's nostrils flared. "Did they ever..." He let the rest trail off. He hadn't wanted to ask, but it would explain so much.

His dad shook his head. "No, thank God. They never touched me or Phil."

Jess breathed a sigh of relief. *What then? What happened here that made you turn out like this?* Jess wanted to ask, but he didn't know if it was one thing or years of many things.

"Do you want to go inside?" he asked the men. They shook their heads.

His dad wandered toward the river. Jess watched him go, his thin frame like a reed, bowed and willowy. Staying a short distance behind, Jess followed. Gus stopped at a fenced-in area dotted with small wooden crosses. Slivers of white paint had peeled off, leaving silver-grey wood behind. The names, painted in black, had faded but were still visible. The gate creaked when his dad opened it. Kneeling down beside a cross at the back of the cemetery, close to the river, Gus reached out a hand to touch it and bowed his head.

"Dad?"

He didn't move, so Jess kneeled beside him. The name on the cross was Phil Sinclair, Gus's brother.

His dad raised his head to the sky and exhaled. "I got to put it right."

"What happened to him?" Jess waited.

It took a long time for his dad to start speaking. "I told Phil we'd leave that night, run back home. So many kids were sick, cholera was taking them out, and the school was a disaster.

Nuns and teachers running around trying to keep the kids quarantined. Us kids wanted our families. It was scary being there with other kids dying."

Jess nodded.

"It was winter. We left in our pajamas and our winter coats. Didn't even have boots, just the school shoes by our bed. So out we go, sneaking past the nuns after they shut off the lights. Got as far as that hill when one of the doctors came in his car and spotted us. I yelled at Phil to split up. I ran toward home. God, it was cold. My feet got numb in the snow and the wind cut through those pajamas like nothing. I thought I was gonna die, I really did." His dad stopped and took a minute to collect himself. Jess could see how hard this was to tell. Each word had to be pulled from the deepest parts of him and dragged out.

"When I got home, I banged on the door and must've collapsed because when I woke up, Ma was there and it was morning. Had frostbite on my toes, ears and fingers. She gave me some kind of bitter tea and let me sleep. I drifted in and out and kept trying to ask about Phil, but the words wouldn't come. Guess I was delirious.

"When a priest from the school showed up, she let him in. Had to. Everyone respected the priests, or feared them. He told her I had to go back with him. Must have said other things too, but whatever it was, she let him take me. I remember crying to her, begging her not to let them take me. She cried too, but shook her head. She had long braids back then and I remember them swinging as she rocked back and forth, crying and moaning."

He stopped, exhausted from the telling, but with another deep breath and a shaking voice, he continued.

"When I got back, they locked me up in the boiler room for the rest of the day and the night. No one said anything about Phil. Figured they'd caught him. It wasn't till I went back to my cot the next day that I saw his bed was empty. I asked the nun who watched us say prayers. 'Where's my brother?' She squinted at me like I'd said a bad thing and sent me back to bed. All night I wondered, was he in the boiler room? Was Ma hiding him? Where'd he go?

"There was one teacher, don't remember his name, wasn't a priest. I asked him if he knew where Phil was. His face got real quiet when he looked at me. 'No one told you?' he asked. 'Your brother died. They found him frozen the morning after you ran away.' Said it as gentle as he could, but I was only eight, didn't make any sense to me. I thought he was lying. Called him names, hit him, ran screaming from him. How could a little kid freeze? Why didn't he keep running?" His voice cracked and he turned toward the river. "Was my fault – my idea to run away. I promised Ma I'd look after him." He didn't bother to wipe away the tears that ran down his face. "Been living with that my whole life," he whispered.

Jess let the words sink in. He shuddered and looked at the weeping man in front of him.

"Dad," he said quietly and took a step closer. "It wasn't your fault."

Gus turned his face up to the sky. A cloud skittered away. The two of them stood in the shadow of the school. *Over thirty years he's been running from this place,* Jess thought. *And he ended up here, anyway.*

CHAPTER 31

MIM BARGED INTO THE KITCHEN, her cheeks glowing from the heat. She had that fiery look in her eyes. I put down my spoon of cereal and waited for her to let loose.

"I just gave Mary Wiens a piece of my mind!"

I let my head fall to the table and groaned. *Oh, God. Rich's mom.* "What did you say?" I mumbled into my arm.

Snorting, she pulled out a chair across from me. "I told her to stop being a gossip and mind her own business. I said, 'You have some nerve, acting like my Sara Jean did wrong to your Rich, when we all know what happened between you and Jim Krahn back in high school.' Well." Mim slapped the table and my spoon clattered out of the bowl. "She turned bright red soon as I mentioned Jim's name and buttoned up her lip and tottled out of the Foodfare so quick, I thought her heels were going to get left behind." She started to cackle, just how she used to when she and Gam would talk. "Serves that busybody right."

"She feels bad for Rich."

Mim shot me a sidelong look. "Feels bad for her reputation more like."

I smiled at the thought of Mim reaming her out in the middle of the grocery store. I'd only seen Mrs. Wiens once since the day at the silo. She'd walked past me as if she didn't know me. All those years we'd spent together, erased.

"Did you really say that to her?"

"Sure did. Poor Jim. Left him as soon as Archie Wiens gave her the time of day! What a commotion that caused. I ever tell you that story?"

I shook my head. "It's not a story, Mim," I reminded her. "It's someone's life."

Mim drew her lips together and surveyed me.

"Rich hasn't answered any of my texts. I think he hates me." I rolled my spoon across the table. Mim's hand reached out and covered mine, stilling it.

"He might. But you'd hate yourself if you had said yes."

I nodded. Her long, spindly fingers squeezed mine.

"I've been meaning to ask you, did you do anything with those letters I gave you?" Mim wasn't much for subtlety. Gam would have hinted and needled but never outright asked.

"I read them."

She rolled her eyes at me. "I figured that. Are you going to find her? Tell her about Gam? Because I was thinking, if you didn't want to, I would." Her admission caught me off guard. I'd been rationing my milestones: break up with boyfriend, start university, contact long-lost mother. Mim was fast-forwarding me.

"Why?"

She uncrossed her legs and leaned closer to me. "I made some decisions in life I'm not proud of. The biggest one is not sticking up for Robyn when I had the chance. I've always regretted that. It wasn't my place. She wasn't my daughter, but I never thought Alice was right in sending her away."

Every night since I read the letters, I thought, *Tomorrow will be the day I call her. Tomorrow I will mail the letter I've written.* It had been a month and tomorrow hadn't come yet.

"My whole life I wanted to know her. But now" – I looked away – "it's like unlocking a door without knowing what's behind it."

What if she didn't want to know me? I was still grieving for Gam, the house a constant reminder of her absence.

Walking past Gam's room got easier every day, but her death hung heavily on me, a shadow over my days, trapping me. When she was alive I'd thought going to school in Winnipeg would make me free, but now I knew that was impossible. No matter where I was, Edelburg would be with me.

Mim and I sat quietly, both lost in our own thoughts. "You expecting anyone?" she asked. I shook my head. "Someone's pulled up out back."

I peeked out the window over the sink. Jess strode toward the steps. Mim craned her neck to see around me as I opened the door and met him in the yard. The last thing I wanted was Mim eavesdropping.

"Hey," he said. He looked tired. There were bags under his eyes and his mouth was drawn in a frown. "Just came by to see how you're doing." He kicked at a stone buried in the ground. When he looked at me, his forehead was wrinkled in concern.

I shrugged. "I'm okay."

He didn't look convinced. "Saw your aunt's car out front."

"Yeah, she's over a lot. She's probably got her ear glued to the screen right now. Mind if we walk down to the garage?"

The door creaked along the track when Jess heaved it open. I remembered the first day of summer vacation, when he'd shown up on my doorstep. It felt like an eternity ago.

Jess's eyes widened at the sight of Gam's medical supplies stuffed in a corner. "When did you – never mind," he said. "Do you want me to take them away, give them to a hospital or something?"

I smiled at him through teary eyes. "Not yet." There was nowhere to sit now that all the boxes had been taken away. "How's your dad?" I asked, leaning against the wall.

"He's okay. Not what I expected. I kinda like him." Jess gave a wry laugh. "That school messed him up," he said quietly, tracing an arc with his foot in the dirt. "We went out there, to the residential school. He told me what happened, about his brother."

As Jess recounted the story of the boys' failed escape, I squeezed my eyes shut. The image of two little boys running blindly through deep snow, scared and desperate, was too hard to bear.

"Did you keep those moccasins?" Jess asked.

I nodded, and a look of relief crossed Jess's face.

"I think I know who they belonged to."

"Was my grandpa..." I let my voice trail off. Part of me didn't want to know the answer. Had he seen how the students suffered? Heard the cries in the boiler room?

Jess shrugged. "Dad told me about a teacher, not a priest, who was kind. It might have been him."

I sat down on the dirt floor and rested my forehead in my hands. Jess jammed his hands into his pockets and stood beside me. "Crazy, eh?"

"Horrible. Your poor dad. Imagine living with that all these years? No wonder –" I caught myself before I finished the rest of the sentence.

"He's an alcoholic?" Jess finished for me and gave a bitter laugh.

A thought tumbled out of my mouth before I could stop it. "Someone should write about it. Tell his story. Maybe if others read it..."

Jess looked at me. "I don't know. He's kept it a secret for so long."

I leaned my head against the wall. "There are so many secrets around here. If people in town knew what had been going on back then, they never would have allowed it."

Jess snorted. "Don't know about that. No one cared what happened to a bunch of Indian kids. They still don't." I'd never heard him sound so despondent, as if he'd given up.

"That's not true," I argued.

"Yeah, it is."

I looked up at him, expecting to see his eyes flash at me in anger. Instead, he shook his head in resignation. "A gang wants in on Deep River. No one cares. There's no RCMP trying to help us. Can you imagine what would happen if they tried to get into Edelburg? Dealing meth behind the library? The Mounties would be here in a second." He paused. "But on a reserve" – he waved a dismissive hand – "who cares? Just a bunch of Indians."

When I stood up, everything started to spin. It was too much. Images flooded my brain: Gam writhing on her bed; the box of letters; I love you, SJ; a little boy frozen in the snow; muffled cries from a boiler room; gang members passing out packages to kids. I felt my knees buckle. If Jess hadn't grabbed me, I would have passed out on the garage floor.

I wished I'd heard his truck outside, or the door slam, but I didn't, and suddenly Rich was in the garage, staring at us with a look of horror. "You're fucking kidding me!"

Adrenaline kicked in, and my lightheadedness disappeared. "What are you doing here?" I asked, panic straining my voice.

He pushed me out of the way and took a step closer to Jess. "What's *he* doing here?" Rounding on me, his eyes narrowed and ugly. When I stayed mute, he advanced, fists clenched at his sides and the tendons in his neck bulging. "What's he *doing* here!" he yelled in my face.

Getting a hold of myself, I planted my feet on the ground. If he wanted to move any closer, he'd have to push me over. "He's working, remember?"

Rich snorted. "Do you think I'm an idiot? Do you think I have no idea what's going on? Everyone talks about it. Everyone knows." His lips curled in distaste, as if I was something filthy. "They've seen the two of you together." He leaned in close and breathed hot, wet breath in my ear. "Did he fuck you?"

I pushed him away, grunting with effort, and let loose a deep, primal scream. "Get out! Get out!"

Rich laughed, catching his balance. He didn't look back at Jess but glared at me as he walked past and spat at my feet.

"You're a whore."

I was shaking, trembling with rage. My face pulsed with heat.

Avoiding Jess's eyes, I sank to the ground and wondered how I could ever have felt anything for Rich. I could hear Jess taking deep, controlled breaths and willed him not to do anything stupid. *Just stay here*, I thought, closing my eyes, *Don't go after him.*

"Hey, asshole!" he shouted, crossing the garage in three strides. I looked up to see Rich turn in time to catch a blow across the chin. The next one landed in his gut, and he doubled over coughing.

"Stop!" I jumped up and raced toward them, grabbing onto Jess's arm and using my body weight to hold him back from throwing another punch. "Stop!"

"What on earth?" Mim clambered down the back stairs, running toward us. She turned a fiery gaze on Jess and walked over to Rich. He stumbled up, gasping for air and still doubled over. "Rich, are you okay?"

He pushed her away. "You're fucking dead!" he yelled at Jess, pointing a shaking hand. "Dead!"

Jess let his arm fall, and I pulled him backwards to the garage, resting a hand on his shoulder. He glared at Rich until he'd got in his truck and peeled away, spraying gravel onto the grass.

Mim stared at me open mouthed.

"Come on," I said, clasping Jess's hand. "It's over."

He shook his head and sighed. "It's just starting."

CHAPTER 32

Jess WALKED INTO THE SCHOOL GYM and sat down. The band meeting had started and a few heads turned as his chair's metal legs scraped against the wooden floor. Chief Duck spoke into the microphone, peering at the crowd through his tinted glasses. He was overweight and his jowls covered his neck. He held the mic too close to his mouth, and each breath echoed in the room, thick with saliva.

"We got to think long-term. Is it the fish that will help our community? Or programs for the young people? If there's no one left on the reserve, there's no one to fish anyhow. We lose a lot of our young people to the city. If we got something here for them, maybe they'll stay." Jess hid a smile. Some of what Chief said had come straight from Kokum's mouth. "We tried to fight against *their* way for a long time. Sometimes it didn't work out so well. Maybe it's time to work together, see what happens."

Someone in the front row raised a hand. Her voice was dwarfed in the gymnasium compared to Chief's magnified one. "It's not working *together*, though. They're taking, same as always."

Chief shook his head. "Not really, Susan. We'd be building it with them. They guarantee half the jobs go to our people. And building the community centre, that's more work for us. We got to do something to keep the young people, eh. Giving them jobs is a start."

"Where's it going to be built? Am I going to look out my

window and see it?" Madeline St. Clair asked. She'd lived on the river her whole life and still trapped in the winter, selling muskrat and rabbit pelts.

Chief shook his head. The microphone rested on his belly and he leaned back in his chair. "Be about ten miles upriver from your place."

"What about flooding? What about my house?" she asked. Suspicion tinged her words.

The Chief hesitated and shifted in his chair. "We'd look at the plans. Make sure as few houses as possible need to be moved."

"I been in that house my whole life. You gonna try and make me move now? Where am I gonna go? Not enough houses as it is." A murmur of voices broke out. The Chief waited until it died down to speak.

"Hydro's offering to build houses for all the people who need to move before they start the dam."

"Bet a Hydro house looks a lot like a trailer," someone muttered.

Jess could feel the mood in the room shifting, the audience losing faith in their chief. Was he a pawn being used by the government? Did he really want to protect their homes, or had the government offered him money to get the band to agree?

Jess stood up, his breath stuck in his throat as he started to speak. "What about the residential school?" *And Tom and all his gang buddies?*

"What about the burial ground? They gonna move that too?" Another member spoke up from the back of the room.

"Ah." Chief hedged his answer. "The school will get torn down. It's in the designated flood area. But the burial grounds are on crown land." Chief Duck hid behind his tinted sun-glasses. "Hydro will only relocate band-owned burial grounds."

Jess looked around. He'd thought the offer to tear down the school would be met with gratitude, a way to erase the pain that still hung over the reserve. But to disrespect the graves of those children? His uncle? That wasn't right.

"Look," Chief held up his hand. "Maybe we can work something out for the burial ground. Remember, Hydro wants to make our community better in exchange for access to our river."

"Not access," Boney shouted. "They're gonna ruin it. No fishing, flooded banks, homes destroyed." People nodded at Boney, who sat down, muttering to himself.

Jess looked at Kokum. Even though she stared impassively ahead, her chest rose and fell quickly, as if she was agitated. He wondered if she'd anticipated such hostility from the crowd. He didn't know any more if the dam was a good thing or not. He thought everyone would be excited to hear about the money and programs the government was willing to offer. Instead, they watched Chief as if he was the enemy, ready to sell them out.

Chief Duck looked relieved when Kokum stood up. She waited until the crowd had quieted before she started speaking, her voice measured and hushed. "Might surprise some of you to know that I think the dam is a good idea. We got to learn from the past. We got to run our reserve like a business. What we got to sell is our resources. We're lucky. Lots of reserves don't have anything, and look at them. Forgotten." She paused, rotating to look at others. "Government might find a way to take the river anyway, and then we get nothing."

Jess wanted to agree with Kokum, but he thought of the legacy of the residential school. The government had convinced First Nations parents to send their kids away so they could get an education and find jobs. Look how that turned out.

"We all got a lot to think about." Chief looked at the clock behind him. "We're gonna table the Hydro issue and move on."

A few people got up to leave, and for the first time Jess noticed Tom's dad sitting across from him at the back of the room. He whispered something to one of his brothers, who also turned to look at Jess.

Seeing them ignited a spark in Jess. Kokum and the others wanted what was best for the reserve, but people like Tom and his family wanted to drag it down. He cleared his throat and stood. "Uh, Chief?"

Chief nodded and leaned back in his chair.

"It's true we got some problems at Deep River for the young people. Like being bored and getting into trouble and that. Like me, eh?" He gave a self-deprecating laugh. "The young people want something to do. Otherwise, sniffing, booze, gangs, you know how it is."

Jess took a deep breath and continued. "Everyone's talking about Hydro coming and how it's gonna ruin Deep River. I think a bigger problem is a gang moving in." He looked pointedly at Tom's dad.

Chief leaned forward on the table, the microphone butting against his chin. "We don't have gangs on Deep River."

"They're coming." A shocked murmur rippled through the crowd. "Some of our members are helping them."

Chief sat at the table, too stunned to say anything.

"You got to send a message. Now, before it gets worse. Anyone living on the reserve who joins a gang, or helps them, isn't a member any more. Gets kicked off."

People started to talk, shocked at the severity of Jess's suggestion. Even someone guilty of murder was still a member of the band. To kick out a member of Deep River was unheard of.

Over in the corner, Tom's dad snorted. "Been breathing in too much of the gasoline you use for the fires, eh?" He and his brother laughed.

Chief ignored them and said to Jess, "Pretty serious punishment." He looked at the elders sitting in front of him. "Don't even know if we can do that."

"Hold on." Tom's dad stood. His voice booming, rough and guttural. "Seeing as how he's not a member, don't think he can bring that up, eh, Chief? How 'bout kicking out an arsonist? Bet he doesn't like that idea, eh?"

"Okay, Monty," Chief said, "calm down." He turned to Jess. "Where'd this come from? You got any specific information about gangs on Deep River?"

Jess nodded, his nostrils flaring as he forced himself not to look at Tom's dad. It was suicidal saying Tom's name out loud, but it was too late now. If he wanted things to be different on Deep River, this was what it would take.

The words were forming on his tongue when the gymnasium door opened and slammed shut. A man ran to the front of the room and grabbed Chief Duck's shoulder. He whispered something urgently in his ear and stood back. Chief grabbed the microphone. "The residential school's on fire." People looked at one another stunned. "There's two crews there now, but it's pretty far gone. We're gonna adjourn the meeting."

Jess looked at Kokum. She stared back. With silent understanding, they both rose to leave.

CHAPTER 33

"LAST NIGHT, A FIRE BURNED out of control at the Edelburg Residential School. Arson is suspected," the newscaster read over the radio. I still flicked it on by habit as soon as I came downstairs in the morning. I liked the company. The house felt too big and empty with just me. I put the cereal box on the counter and turned up the volume.

"The building, vacant at the time, was shut down in 1983 after operating as a residential school for First Nations children since 1921. 'At this time, we are asking anyone with information to come forward,' says RCMP Constable Miller. This is the fifth case of arson in the Deep River Valley since March."

The newscaster moved on to a farming report, and I turned the knob so the voice became a low hum. A hard knot formed in my chest. Had Jess set the fire?

The moccasins sat on the counter, on top of the attendance ledger, photographs and letter. I'd planned on returning them to him today. Like the letters Gam had kept from me, all of it needed to go back to where it belonged. I'd never know why Grandpa hadn't sent the letter and had kept the moccasins. Guilt? Fear? He could have tracked Gus down; they'd only lived a few miles from each other.

My stomach churned. It was time for things to be made right again. No more secrets boxed up and hidden.

But if Jess did have a part in the fire, what then? He was still on probation for the last time he got caught. No judge would let him walk away with community service hours. He'd get jail time.

No longer hungry, I left the bowl on the counter and wandered to the kitchen window. The car was parked on the grass, washed and ready for a drive into the city. Last night, I'd gone to sleep excited about buying my university books, but the feeling was slowly leaking away.

The phone rang and I grabbed it, forgetting that a ringing phone wouldn't wake anyone else. It was just me. "Hello?"

"Is Sara Jean there, please?" The voice sounded breathy and the words came out quickly.

"Speaking."

"Oh." She faltered and her voice cracked. "Sara Jean, it's Robyn…your mother." She sobbed the last words, overcome with emotion. I gripped the table and let the words sink in. I had to sit down.

Sniffling, she started speaking again. "Aunt Mim sent me a letter. She told me everything. I had to call to let you know I'm here and how much I want to see you. When you're ready."

I sat mute at the kitchen table. My ears strained for the sound of her breath in the receiver. All the things I'd imagined saying to her vanished. "I – I." I stammered. "There's so much…"

"I know," she sighed. "It's overwhelming."

"Yeah," I whispered and clutched the receiver to my ear, desperate to hang on to her. "Gam told me some things just before she…when she was in the hospital."

"I can't imagine what it was like, losing her. I am so, so sorry, Sara Jean."

"She told me you had other kids and that you lived in Winnipeg. All this time, you were so close." I was surprised at the accusatory tone of my voice.

There was a pause. I'd been a car ride away. In a few hours, she could have been at the front door. What had held her back? Was it really Gam, or was it the simplicity of the life she'd made for herself in Winnipeg? One that would be complicated by her teenage daughter in Edelburg? A flush of anger rose up my neck, and tears prickled behind my eyes.

"I didn't know if you'd see me. I wrote letters for so long and then...I just couldn't any more. It was too hard. Never hearing anything back." She took a breath and calmed herself. "You have a sister and brother. Taylor is eight and Dylan is ten. I hope you can meet them one day."

"Do they know about me?"

She cleared her throat, "No, I – I," she stammered an explanation. "They're too young. They wouldn't understand why I left you."

I closed my eyes against her words. *That makes three of us.*

"I wanted to have this conversation in person, not over the phone." Her voice was gentle. I wondered if she was a good mother to her children. "Do you think you'd meet me somewhere, for coffee maybe? I want to get to know you. Mim says you're an amazing, kind, beautiful girl."

Tears sprang to my eyes. I could hear the pain in her voice. How many times had I wished for my mom to say those words? "I'll think about it," I said. "You know, I'm the same age as you were when you had me."

"I know."

"I know how Gam could be. And what it's like in Edelburg. But you had a choice. You should have fought harder for me."

"I know," she whispered.

There was nothing more to say, not right now. "I'll think about it, meeting you. But –"

"Okay," she interrupted, quick to agree. "Anytime. Or another time on the phone, we could talk. Get to know each other." There was hope in her voice. "Can I give you my number?"

A lump rose in my throat as I wrote it down.

"Good-bye, Sara Jean," she said.

"Bye" My breath stalled in my throat. What should I call her? Mom? Robyn? The quiet dangled between us until the dial tone sounded in my ear. My breath came in shaky spurts after we hung up. I stared at the paper with her number on it, letting the sound of her voice echo in my head.

Mim arrived a few minutes later, punctual as always for her nine a.m. check-up on me. "Morning," she said when she walked in. "Sara Jean?" she asked, taking a second look at me.

No point in hiding the truth from her. She'd probably pull out a forensics kit, looking for answers anyway. "My mom just called me."

Mim pulled out a chair and sat across from me. Her bare legs squelched against the vinyl seat. "That's great!"

"You wrote to her?" I said, my voice heavy with accusation. She met my eyes. "I had to. I never should have let her leave."

"It wasn't up to you."

"But she's your mother!" She stared at me incredulously.

"It's my decision! All my life I've done what Gam wanted, living here, in this town. I've been trapped in this house for eighteen years, looking after her! Let me have a taste of what it's like to make my own decisions."

Mim puckered her mouth and raised her eyebrows at me. I had never raised my voice before, but it felt good, as if the chains that bound me were being loosened.

"I was trying to do what was best for you –"

"Like Gam?" I interrupted. Mim bit back whatever else she was going to say and stared across the table at me. "I don't need you to take over for her."

"Fine," Mim said. She started to fidget. "I have to get to the grocery store. Tomatoes are on for ninety-nine cents a pound. I'll pick some up for –" She broke off. "Never mind" She looked bothered. "I guess I can be a bit overbearing."

"I'm going to the city to buy my books today," I told her as she opened the screen door.

"Oh?" She turned back, her eyebrows raised in surprise. "You didn't say. When did you decide that?"

I sighed. "Does it matter?"

"No. I guess not." She came back to the table, grabbed my hand and gave it a squeeze. Her pointy, painted nails grazed my wrist. "So that means…" She let her voice trail off, drawing her own conclusions.

I nodded. "School starts in a week."

Mim raised her eyebrows, giving her head a little shake. She didn't look upset, just surprised. I caught myself before I apologized. It didn't matter if I disappointed her. I was finally making choices for myself.

"Call me when you're home. I want to hear all about it."

"I will," I agreed and glanced at the clock. "I should get going. Long drive."

The screen door clapped shut after her. In front of me was the phone number. I picked up the pencil and wrote *Mom* above it and stuck it to the fridge with a magnet. My chest swelled with emotion as I stood in the kitchen, staring at it.

You are alone.

Not any more.

CHAPTER 34

KOKUM SHOOK HER HEAD as she looked at the rubble. The school had almost burned to the ground. Three brick walls blackened with soot and a few charred posts were all that remained. Jess walked closer to the site, the smell of smoke still heavy in the air. His shoes and jeans were coated in ash from the ground. The old building had gone up like straw. He could almost hear the thunderous collapse of the roof as it fell down into the blaze below and was swallowed by hungry flames.

Jess had borrowed Boney's car that morning to drive out, curious to see what was left of the school.

"Comin' with you," his kokum had said, her face impassive. He hadn't argued. Once the rubble was bulldozed into the ground there'd be nothing left, nothing to remind people of the Edelburg Residential School. At least, nothing anyone could see.

He'd never set a fire this big. Sheds, dumpsters, garbage cans, his fires were small, easy to walk away from. His fires were about gaining control, not destruction. Did that make him a better firebug? He gave a wry smile at the thought and wondered if one person or a group had set the fire. Was a rival gang trying to send a message?

Kokum wandered off toward the river – toward the burial ground. The fire had left the crosses untouched. They stood weathered and silvery in the morning sun. She stared out at the crosses crowded together. Tiny coffins don't take up much space. "You okay?" Jess asked, coming up behind her.

"Never been here before," she mumbled in her musical cadence, the last syllable lifting like it was a question.

Jess made a noise in his throat. "Come on. I'll show you."

Phil's name had been re-painted. The letters stark and black against the cross. Some dried wild flowers, their heads yellowed and bent in submission, lay strewn across the grave. Kokum closed her eyes and swayed beside Jess. A breeze picked up, whirling the flowers around. From deep inside her throat, his grandmother started to hum and then opened her mouth to let the sounds spill out. A deep, mournful cry filled the air and was lifted by the wind. Jess had never heard the mourning cry before and barely breathed as the sounds carried him away from the burial ground, the school, the reserve.

The moment was broken by the sound of a car grinding gravel under its tires. Kokum's mouth shut and she bowed her head, swallowing the remaining notes.

Jess moved up the hill to get a better look at who had arrived. If it was cops, it would look suspicious for him to be hanging around. But it wasn't a cruiser, it was a familiar white truck parked like a beacon at the top of the hill. Jess felt his shoulders tighten as Rich stood on the running board surveying the remains of the school.

A taunting smile spread over Rich's face when he caught sight of Jess. "Visiting the scene of the crime?"

Jess didn't say anything.

He walked toward Jess. "Found out from my cousin what you got busted for." He shook his head mockingly. "Arson. Does Sara Jean know that's what you do for fun?"

For the first time, Jess noticed that Rich wasn't alone. Two other guys sat in the front seat and as Rich moved down the hill, they got out of the truck. The three of them advanced toward him, and Jess gritted his teeth. It had been inevitable, this confrontation. Typical of a townie to make it three against one.

"Not so tough now, are you?"

"You brought two friends," Jess pointed out. Rich was a lightweight, and one friend looked doughy, even though he was big. The third one was in the best shape, but he didn't look like he wanted to be here and kept throwing worried glances at Rich.

The townies were only a few feet away from him, and despite trying not to look intimidated, Jess could feel his heart racing. Planting his feet and lowering his centre of gravity, he locked eyes with Rich. He didn't turn to look at Kokum and wasn't sure if Rich and his friends had realized she was there.

"You'll probably go to jail for this fire. No judge would let you go on community service after this one. Poor Sara Jean. What will she do without you to protect her?" A sick smile twisted Rich's face.

"You gonna throw a punch, or just talk?" Jess bore down, ready for the first blow. Rich was on the right and the doughy kid was in the middle. Tactial error. Jess would easily take that kid down with a punch to the gut. He had no muscles to protect his stomach and kidneys. Jess realized these townies had probably never fought before.

Winding up, Jess's fist landed into the meaty softness of the middle kid's stomach. With a gasp and a cough, he stopped walking, holding his side. Rich looked at him with disgust and swung at Jess, who easily dodged the punch. Jess felt his knuckles connect with Rich's cheekbone. The impact of bone on bone sent a jolt up his arm. Rich's head flew back and he staggered, holding his face. Jess stayed on his toes, his fists ready. Rich gave a half-hearted swing, opening up his side, and Jess caught him in the ribs. "Do something!" Rich gasped to his friends as he swayed on his feet.

The doughy kid moved in, but Jess got low and landed another punch to his side and the kid went down. The third kid took a look at his friends and backed off. "I just wanted to look at the building, man. I never knew we were here to fight."

Jess laughed. "You call this a fight?" He let his fists fall. "Get the hell out of here." He watched as the three of them backed away to the truck. Rich's face was swelling already. The shiner he'd wake up with tomorrow would be a fitting souvenir of his time at the residential school.

Unclenching his fist, Jess felt a stinging soreness throb through his hand. Once the truck had driven away, he turned to Kokum. She shook her head and walked toward him. "Think you made it worse. Shoulda let him hit you once. Get it out of his system, eh?"

She was probably right. Rich was going to keep coming after him until he'd gotten his pound of flesh. Would he take his frustration out on Sara Jean? He'd said her name like she was something dirty. "Can we get going? I need to take you home. There's something I have to do." He hoped he was being paranoid or that Sara Jean had picked today to go to the city, but he pressed the gas pedal hard and flew down the gravel road, the remains of the residential school shrinking away to nothing in the rearview mirror.

CHAPTER 35

THE INSISTENT KNOCKING ON THE SCREEN DOOR made me jump. I peered out my bedroom window, but whoever it was there was hidden by the overhang.

"Hold on," I muttered and finished getting dressed. Glancing at the time, I groaned. I needed to get on the road soon to arrive in Winnipeg before lunch.

When I got downstairs, the back porch was empty. I looked around the yard. An unfamiliar brown four-door idled by the garage. I walked down the steps. "Hello?"

As I rounded the corner to the front, so did Jess, and we collided. "What's going on?" I asked. He looked flustered, his cheeks crimson and his eyes wide and darting.

He ran a hand through his hair. "Gah! Where were you? I was banging on the door."

I stared at him, confused. Why was he so panicked?

Moving closer, he put his hand behind my head and pulled me toward him. I could feel his heart pounding against his ribcage. The cotton of his T-shirt was damp and sticky against his skin. A sweet, smoky smell clung to him.

"Rich never came by?"

"Rich?" I raised an eyebrow. "No. Why?"

He gave a half-hearted laugh. "He said something that made me think he might. He was just playing me, though." He shook his head. "That guy is such an asshole."

I narrowed my eyes. "Where'd you see him?"

He hesitated. "Did you hear about the residential school?"

I tried to take a breath, but the air got stuck in my throat. *Please, please don't tell me you did it.* I nodded. "On the radio this morning."

"I wanted to see what was left. And check on the burial ground."

I nodded, waiting for him to continue. I still didn't know how Rich figured into all this.

"Rich showed up with some loser friends of his."

I rolled my eyes. I gave Jess a quick once-over. He didn't have any obvious injuries, and then I noticed his hand. His knuckles were red and swollen. "What happened?" I asked, reaching for his fingers.

He shrugged it off. "Landed a few punches on some big, flabby guy."

"Jordan Dirks," I said.

"And Rich."

I bit back a smile. Rich deserved at least a black eye. I hoped it was a good punch that had left him reeling.

"Your car," I said, nodding toward it. "It's still running."

"Oh shit, right."

What had Rich said to make him race over here and pound on my door? He was probably right, Rich was just playing him. He'd always known what to say to hurt my feelings or make me feel guilty. Kind of ironic that Rich's comment, whatever it was, was pushing Jess and me closer.

"You going somewhere?" Jess asked. I'd blow-dried my hair, so instead of being pulled into a haphazard ponytail, it hung sleekly to my shoulders. I'd also put on makeup and some jewellery: thin metal bracelets that jingled on my arm.

"To Winnipeg. I'm going to buy my university books."

I opened my mouth to tell him about my mom's phone call that morning, but a car with flashing police lights pulled up beside Jess's brown four-door. Two officers got out, checked the license plate and walked over to us. One kept his hand on a taser in its holster.

"Jess Sinclair?" one of them asked.

My body tensed, and I looked at Jess.

"You're under arrest for arson and possession of flammable materials with the intent to commit arson." The officer, Chris, a cousin of Rich's, held out handcuffs and walked behind Jess, clicking them into place.

Jess looked at me, his face pale. He looked like a trapped animal, eyes wide and scared, as he struggled against the cuffs, even though there was no way out of them.

"Is this about the residential school?" I asked Chris. He was a good guy, but he was Rich's cousin.

"Stay out of it, Sara Jean." The warning tone in Chris's voice should have shut me up, but I believed Jess. "Chris, wait! There's a mistake. He didn't do it."

Chris handed Jess off to his partner and walked over to me. In a low voice he said, "I don't know what you're doing with this punk, but you got to stay away from him." He leaned in so we were standing ear to ear. "We checked out his trailer and found all the evidence we need."

"What are you talking about?" I narrowed my eyes at Chris. "What did you find?"

He hesitated, probably worried about breaking some rule by telling me. "Chris?" I prompted.

"Gasoline, rags, a lighter. Right under his trailer," he whispered. "I'm telling you, this guy is dangerous."

Biting my lip, I looked at Jess. He was shaking his head and muttering. I could see smears of white powdery ash on his jeans. A ball of nausea rolled up in my stomach. I felt like a fool. All these weeks, telling secrets and confessions to someone I barely knew.

Jess started to struggle and jerk his elbows around. "This is bullshit! It wasn't me!"

The officer held the top of Jess's head, forcing him to duck into the backseat of the police car. Chris slammed the passenger door and walked around to the driver side. Before he got in the car, he threw me a warning look.

Jess slouched down in the backseat as they drove away, lights flashing. Like a lost child, I didn't know what to do or where to turn.

My car was parked inside the garage. If I wanted to go buy books, I should leave, go to the city. It was time to start my life, not stick around and try to help a guy I barely knew. What could I even do? If he was guilty, I'd look like a gullible fool.

I wanted my freedom, to leave Edelburg and make my own decisions. Even if they were the wrong ones, at least they'd be mine. My car sat in the garage, waiting. I ran inside and grabbed my keys. The moccasins sat on the counter. I hesitated, my breath caught in my throat. I needed to go.

The car hummed to life. I put it in reverse and backed out of the driveway. When I pulled up to the highway exit, my foot sat on the brake. Left to Winnipeg, right to Deep River Reserve.

Pushing the signal lever up, I turned right.

The homes were stretched far apart, with nothing but flat, grassy land between. A few had flowerpots and vegetable gardens, but there were lots of bicycles and hockey nets littering yards. Dogs roamed the street, some keeping pace alongside the car.

I asked at the gas station where Jess's grandmother, Mrs. Sinclair, lived. The kid behind the counter looked up from his magazine and eyed me warily. "I'm friends with Jess," I told him, trying to keep the impatience out of my voice.

"Keep going down this road and turn left at the four-way. She's the third on the right, got a wood pile in front."

"Thank you," I said and ran back to the car.

A pickup and another car were already parked haphazardly in front of the house. The first hurdle had been to find out where Jess's grandmother lived. Now that I'd done that, I had no idea how to explain why I'd come to her house. Should I barge in like Aunt Mim: "You don't know me, but your grandson's been arrested for arson?" Or should I ask her to step outside so we could speak privately? Would she believe me, or would she look at me like the kid at the gas station had?

Then I remembered the look on Jess's face when Chris had shown up. I walked to the door.

Through the glass, I could see a group of six people, all men and one woman, sitting in a circle on couches and chairs. I tapped gently on the glass. A few faces turned. "Come in," someone called.

I ignored the curious stares and cleared my throat. "Are you Jess's kokum?" I asked the woman. Her hair, shot with grey, was pulled back into a tight bun at the nape of her neck. I glanced at her feet. She wore a pair of moccasins with a familiar beaded design.

She nodded but didn't get up. I walked around the room and crouched beside her. "Jess is in trouble." The words tumbled out of my mouth. "He's at the police station in town."

She made a noise in her throat, the same noise I'd heard Jess make. "*Humpf.* What for?"

"For the fire at the residential school." I said it quietly, trying to keep our conversation private, but in the silent room, there weren't any secrets.

"He was at the meeting when it went up," she said and turned to the group.

"They found rags and gasoline under his trailer." I felt like a traitor for saying the words out loud. Sticking her bottom lip out, she turned to the man next to her. He looked like he was eighty years old, with missing teeth and patchy whiskers poking through his lined skin. "Boney, you go find Gus, eh? Tell him to get to the police station in town." The man nodded and didn't ask any questions.

As Boney stood up to go, Jess's grandmother met my eyes and nodded. "You didn't have to come. A lot of people wouldn't."

I looked away, embarrassed to admit that I almost hadn't.

CHAPTER 36

SITTING ON THE HARD WOODEN BENCH for the past few hours had made Jess's ass numb. He kept shifting, trying to bring some feeling back into his tailbone. The three officers at the station ignored him as they buzzed around the office answering the phone, checking files, clicking at the computer keys and pouring burnt coffee into stained mugs. Jess had stopped trying to make eye contact with them; this was their game. To make sure he knew who was in control. Instead, he hung his head and let his shoulders slump. Maybe if they thought he'd given up, they'd talk to him.

The door to the station swung open, and a man stumbled in. His jeans were filthy and ripped at the knees. Silvery hair stood up in spiky tufts and his skin had a pale yellow hue to it. Jess froze.

"I'd like to 'fess. Was me," the man slurred and grabbed onto a chair to stay upright. An officer came over and eased him onto the chair. "Sir? Are you drunk, sir?" Jess saw the other one, the one who knew Sara Jean, roll his eyes at his partner.

"'S my son. My baby boy there." He pointed a trembling hand at Jess, who closed his eyes and shook his head.

"Sir? Sir?" The officer stood directly in front of Gus, trying to get his attention. "Do you know where you are?"

"At the pleece station. 'Sokay, son. I did it. I'm here to cofess." Gus tried to focus on Jess, but his eyes rolled around the officer standing beside him.

"For what? What did you do?" the officer asked.

"Burned it down!" He let out a whoop of laughter. "Bloody building! My baby brother died, y'know that? School killed 'im."

The officers looked at each other, puzzled. Rich's cousin went to Gus, but the other one walked over to Jess. "Is that your father?"

Jess nodded.

"He claims that he set the fire at the school."

Jess shrugged. "He's a drunk."

The officer licked his lips. "I can see that."

Gus had started sobbing. "Lemme talk to him." He tried to stand, but the officer restrained him. Gus fought against him. "He's my boy. Let go of me!" The officer forced Gus to sit down, but Gus starting ranting. "It wasn't him, it was me! I hated that school. Went back last night and lit it up like a fucking bonfire. Watched it burn till I heard the trucks comin' and then left."

"He's drunk," Jess shouted. "He doesn't know what he's saying." Jess had never seen his father like this. He remembered him as a silent and depressed drunk, not a loud and sloppy one.

"Stashed the rags and shit under the trailer, was gonna get rid of 'em today." He melted into a sobbing heap on the chair.

Two officers exchanged a glance.

Jess narrowed his eyes at his father. Rags under the trailer? What was he talking about? All his supplies were safely hidden in the hole he'd dug.

"You willing to sign a statement?" asked the officer.

"Dad? What the hell are you doing?" Jess shouted across the room. All the officers turned to him.

"Thas the first time" – he took a breath – "you called me Dad." He gave a little laugh and met Jess's eyes.

Jess stared at him. "What are you doing?" Gus bent his head and looked away. "He didn't do it! He's lying," Jess shouted. Tears prickled behind his eyes as he twisted his hands, desperate to get out of the handcuffs. "Dad, I didn't set fire to the school, I swear!"

A look of doubt crossed Gus's face. But it was replaced by resignation. "Waz takin' so long?" he slurred. "Only got a few weeks to live." He looked up at them with a hangdog expression. "Liver cancer. Gonna die soon." The officer narrowed his eyes with disbelief.

Gus's head wobbled on his neck as he tried to focus on the officer. "You gonna let my kid go?"

Jess held his breath and squeezed his fists together. The metal handcuffs dug into his wrists. Jess trembled with a new kind of anger. His dad was going to be locked up for the last few weeks of his pitiful life. He turned away, unable to look at him any more.

The officer nodded. "Your kid's got an alibi, corroborated by Chief Duck. If you're saying you did it, we can't keep him," he said and hoisted Gus to his feet. "Let's get you inside to sober up."

Gus shuffled past. Jess could feel his eyes on him but refused to meet them. He was throwing away his last chance to be a father by trying to be a hero.

KOKUM SAT ON THE FRONT STEPS of her house. A chipmunk danced around, tracking the bread crumbs she tossed to it. Jess had walked to the edge of town and then hitched a ride to the reserve. He hadn't eaten all day and dragged his feet across her yard. The late afternoon sun reflecting in the front windows blinded him.

Jess sat down beside her. "I didn't do it. He's going to go to jail because he thinks I burned down that fucking school!" All the venom that had been stirring in Jess since he left the station spilled out with his tears. He closed his eyes against the image of his dad, tinged yellow by the cancer and cuffed, the cops towering over him.

Kokum shook her head. She moved imperceptibly closer to him.

"He's going to die in jail," Jess mumbled.

Kokum gave a resigned sigh and nodded her head. She reached behind her. "Your friend came by. Brought these back to me." In her hands were the moccasins. "Told me how you found them. Each of my boys had a pair. These were Phil's." She rubbed a loving hand over the hide.

Sara Jean had been here.

"Brought this back too." A blue folder lay on the steps. Jess opened it. Sara Jean had signed off on hours for every day since he'd met her. Double what he'd actually worked. His throat tightened as he closed the folder.

Kokum stuck out her bottom lip. The chipmunk, no longer being fed, scolded her and scampered away. "Gus told me about Phil last night, before the band meeting. Hard to hear, even now." She took a breath and clasped her hands in her lap. Tears leaked out the corners of her eyes. "Glad I got these back," she said. Her hand trembled. "He woulda burned that school down if he had the guts."

Jess shook his head. For once his kokum was wrong. "He has guts."

She slipped her warm, weathered hand in his.

"He acted drunk at the station," Jess told her.

"Boney's idea. Give him a defense in case he makes it to trial."

A cricket jumped across the yard, propelling itself a few inches each time. Jess remembered scurrying around after them when he was a kid, trying to catch one to put in a jar. He learned quickly that once it was captured, it wasn't fun any more. Not much room for a grasshopper to jump in a jar. "Gang'll have to find a new base. Slow 'em down a bit."

Kokum nodded. "Elders had a meeting this morning. Gonna advise Chief to pass your idea about people helping the gangs."

Jess raised an eyebrow. "That was fast."

"Tom's gone. His uncle said he went to the city."

"He'll be back."

Kokum nodded. "Hydro wants to meet with the elders. Want you to be there too. Need a young person's voice."

The setting sun cast an orange glow behind a band of clouds.

"How can I make it better here?"

She looked at him a long time and finally said, "Stay."

CHAPTER 37

THE HIGHWAY STRETCHED IN FRONT OF ME like a concrete ribbon weaving through the fields. I'd opened the window a crack, and the wind crackled and roared in my ear, drowning out the radio. I glanced over at the books on the passenger seat, and a glow of satisfaction spread through me.

Even as I drove to Edelburg, the tangible reality that I was free, I could leave, made me shiver with excitement. I'd drive back and forth to university until I found a place to live. Then I'd come back once in a while on weekends to check on the house. Maybe I'd sell it or rent it out. Mim would help. But soon I'd leave Edelburg behind and make my life in Winnipeg.

I thought of my mom as I drove. I could invite her over to see my apartment, or my dorm room. The tearful reunion I thought would never happen, would. We'd have a shaky beginning at first, full of hiccups and awkward, guilt-filled silences. But over the years, a bond would grow, and we'd be able to look at each other without any silent accusations or apologies.

And I would write about it – all of it. It would be my story to tell.

ACKNOWLEDGEMENTS

FIRST OF ALL, I would like to thank my family, especially my "indirectly helpful" husband (his words, not mine) and my boys, James and Thomas. A lot of determination and hard work goes into writing, but it is only possible with the love and support of those around me.

My sister, Nancy Chappell-Pollack, is my best and favourite reader because she doesn't shy away from telling me the truth. I appreciate the time you give to reading and commenting on my books – often suffering through some horrendous first drafts!

I am fortunate to have supportive siblings and parents. Thank you to Karen Deeley, Gordon Chappell, Chuck Chappell and, of course, my mom, to whom the book is dedicated.

Thank you also to Sacha Nelson and Kathy Tarrant, both early readers of this book, and Rocky Pollack for his judicial fact-checking services. (Any errors in the text are mine!)

Finally, I would like to thank Kathryn Cole, my insightful editor, and the wonderful team at Coteau Books. It has been a pleasure to work with all of you.

ABOUT THE AUTHOR

COLLEEN NELSON is the author of two other young adult novels, *Tori by Design*, winner of the 2012 McNally Robinson Book of the Year for Young People Award, and *The Fall*, winner of the 2014 McNally Robinson Book of the Year for Young People Award, selected as a CCBC "Best Book for Teens" and nominated for the OLA's 2014 White Pine Award.

Colleen has lived in Japan and New York City but currently calls Winnipeg home.